Crystal Lake Inn

Susan W. Green

CRYSTAL LAKE INN

Copyright © 2021 Susan W. Green

ISBN: 979-8-9853114-0-2

CHAPTER 1

Cassidy was a bit frazzled. It wasn't her typical way to approach a full house at her country inn, but her chef had a family emergency and had to go out of town for a few weeks. This left Cassidy alone to keep everything on schedule and running smoothly.

She sent a text to her two best friends with an emergency emoji, the image of a life preserver, indicating she desperately needed their help. While Cassidy waited for them to arrive, she checked that the coffee bar was fully stocked and the buffet table was loaded with plates, silverware, napkins, juice, cups, and glasses.

As she started to walk back into the kitchen she heard a familiar sound outside. Walking over to one of the large windows overlooking the inn's front lawn, she paused to watch as her friend Trish got off her motorcycle, pulled her long platinum blond hair into a ponytail, put her riding gloves in her saddlebag, and strapped her helmet to the seat. Trish was fairly conservative, and it often caught people off-guard to see such a petite woman riding a motorcycle. Yet, it was the easiest way to get around town, especially during tourist season. Trish owned a local gift shop on Main Street and fortunately employed a terrific store manager so she could come to the aid of her friend when needed.

Trish looked up at Cassidy through the window and gave a big wave as she hustled up the walkway to the front door.

Cassidy took a moment to gaze across the lawn and beyond to the water, which was gleaming brightly from the sun that was just starting to come fully awake—and then she caught her reflection in the large front window. She saw a slender and physically fit woman in her early thirties. Running a multi-story inn kept her in good shape and she often logged over forty-thousand steps a week on the step-tracker app on her watch. Her long light brown hair was straight and fell half-way down her back. She felt fortunate her hair had natural highlights that got even lighter in the summer. But her dark brown eyes were her best feature. They were surrounded by thick long dark brown eyelashes. People often complimented Cassidy on her eyes, saying they were doe-like.

Over the years several people had said she looked like a younger version of the actress, Jennifer Love Hewitt. Personally, she didn't see the resemblance, but she tried to take the compliment in stride.

Thinking about compliments on her personal appearance was a touchy subject for Cassidy. She shuddered when she thought back to the constant flow of compliments Ben had paid her.

Handsome and built like a football player, Ben was her college sweetheart. They started out as friends but over the course of their junior year their relationship started to get more serious. They were both majoring in business at the University of Southern Maine at the campus in Portland. They had a lot of the same classes and partnered for several research projects. By the fall of their senior year, they were both thinking about a future together. On Christmas Day, six months before graduation and in front of Cassidy's family, Ben proposed, and she said yes.

Cassidy was floating on air as she returned to classes in January but was super busy. On top of finishing her last semester, she was also trying to plan a wedding to take place in mid-June just after finals and graduation. She was so focused on her classwork and preoccupied with the plans for the big day that she failed to notice that, at some point in the early spring, Ben didn't seem to be as excited about the wedding as she was. Cassidy assumed that was just the way it was supposed to be—the woman was always more excited about the frilly details of the wedding than the man.

As the weeks went by and school and the wedding plans got more and more hectic, Cassidy suddenly realized that Ben wasn't as attentive or as loving as he used to be. She started to feel that something wasn't right and asked him several times if anything was wrong. But Ben always gave her a bright smile, kept the compliments flowing and said everything was "fine".

Everything was fine—until it wasn't. A week before the invitations went out for the wedding and in the middle of spring exams, Ben told Cassidy that he was terribly sorry, but he couldn't marry her. The engagement was off.

The short of the long painful story was that Ben fell in love with someone else. It seemed he'd been seeing someone from a rival university and he unexpectantly fell in love with her. He had planned to break it off with the other woman but there was a child expected in the fall and Ben's family insisted he do right by the other woman. They had gotten married by the Justice of the Peace the weekend before he finally told her.

Cassidy was the last to know. She was heartbroken, but more than that she was furious that she let all the compliments and smiles fool her into a false sense of security and love. She was now a hundred-year-old cliché— the woman was always 'the last to know'.

Embarrassed and devastated, she struggled to finish the last three months of school. She pulled away from her family and friends and mainly hid in her dorm room. Being too proud to fail, she put all her effort into her classes and managed to graduate with honors.

Now, when her mother or her friends gave her grief about not dating, she just looked them straight in the eye for a minute and then said one word to them… "Ben". That typically got them to quickly change the subject.

For years now Cassidy had only casually dated. That allowed her to protect her heart. But, as the years went on, she wondered if she was missing something. Would she ever find 'Mr. Right'? Was it in her future to get married, have children and a white picket-fence?

Working hard to get the inn running smoothly took the vast majority of her time and left little to no space in her schedule for dating or for beauty treatments at the salon. Her focus, from her perspective, was spot on…the inn was her life.

Those who knew her best often said that Cassidy Taylor failed to see her own beauty and did little to make her personal life a priority.

Cassidy was known for giving back to the community and served on several committees for projects that supported the town and local small businesses like the downtown restoration she helped shepherd three years ago. The little town of Lakeview was thriving.

And of course, it was a reciprocal relationship for Cassidy's inn. Lakeview, Maine was famous for its many lakes and mountains and the Crystal Lake Inn took full advantage of what the town had to offer. The inn sat on the outskirts of the small town and was nestled between Crystal Lake in the front and the Pineview Mountains in the back. It was a beautiful two-story structure that had been expanded over the years with the addition of ten large guest rooms, each with its own bathroom, small kitchenette, and a view of either the lake or the majestic mountains. The traditional white building had a pitched roof, gables at each end and a series of dormers running across the second floor.

The winding paved front walkway led along gorgeous flowerbeds to the front porch, which was one of the inn's best features. The porch wrapped around three sides of the first floor of the building and was deep enough to hold lots of comfortable wicker furniture with overstuffed cushions. A set of double mahogany doors set the stage for the décor inside the inn, which was mainly antiques Cassidy collected over the years from local shops and a few handmade pieces from local craftsmen.

Crystal Lake Inn was a repeat favorite and many of its guests booked routinely year after year. Surrounded by beautiful gardens, well-lit walkways and places to sit and relax, the inn was as beautiful on the outside as it was on the inside. The structure, which started out as a typical two-story clapboard family home, sat on a large piece of land, and the two major additions done over the years made it look more like a country manor house than a typical New England home.

Cassidy never got tired of the breathtaking views and it often reminded her that she almost missed out on owning the inn.

Still standing in front of the large picture window in the community room, Cassidy stared out at the gorgeous spring day with its cloudless blue skies, trees starting to bloom and weather warm enough for the early risers to take their morning walk without a jacket.

Yet Cassidy felt a slight chill run down her arms as her thoughts drifted back to that Autumn day five years ago…in her mind she could clearly see the beautiful fall scenery that graced the path around the lake as she strolled along one of the forest trails that lay beyond, hear the crunch of the gently fallen leaves beneath her shoes and smell the earthiness of the undergrowth.

So many emotions ran through Cassidy's mind as she thought about her grandmother, known as Grams by her family. Cassidy and Grams had always been close. Grams had been the one to help Cassidy through her grief after her father died when she was a young teen. They had become almost inseparable since Cassidy's mother struggled to deal with her own deep grief and had another younger daughter, Jennifer, still at home.

On that fall day, Cassidy and Grams had met at their favorite place at the lake for a picnic lunch. Cassidy was a bit early so she sat down on the cement bench near the walkway to take in the view of the beauty surrounding her. The leaves were so vividly aglow that it almost seemed like they were on fire.

Cassidy's mind was buzzing. She was so excited to share her dream with Grams. A dream that started with a blank page, yet grew over the years, piece by piece, until she now had a full picture in her mind and a business plan down on paper. She had her finances in order due in part to a small inheritance from a great aunt, and she couldn't wait to get started. Cassidy had decided to buy, remodel and reopen the inn.

Many years ago, the inn was a beautiful and stately private home. Over time it had changed hands and the last surviving member of the original owner's family bought the property and turned it into an inn. For decades it was a popular local spot for dining and for vacationing families but eventually the owner's failing health translated into the inn falling into shambles, and the lack of maintenance took its toll on the structure and grounds.

When Cassidy saw an ad in the local newspaper announcing the inn was going up for auction, she knew it was the perfect opportunity for her. Cassidy made the best bid she could afford on auction day and she was overjoyed when the inn became hers. That is, until she realized just how much work it entailed.

The inspection revealed that the building needed not only décor updates, but structural improvements. That included tearing down and totally rebuilding the front porch, which Cassidy always thought was one of the inn's best features since it faced the lake. Having to rebuild the porch was expensive but it also turned out to be a blessing. Once the porch was demolished, the contractor told Cassidy that he could rebuild it so it would be even more usable and lovely than it had been before. She envisioned lots of rockers, a large porch swing, small bistro tables and a place to host guests every evening—and that vision became reality.

Cassidy also quickly realized that she needed help beyond the construction crew. She desperately needed someone with decorating experience, and she just happened to know the best person for the job—and invited her grandmother to lunch.

Cassidy stood up to hug Grams as she approached the bench. She opened the picnic hamper, offered Grams a sandwich and asked her for updates on several of the charities her grandmother supported. The two talked and laughed for several minutes and then Grams said, "OK Cassidy. What's up? I can tell when you have something on your mind." Cassidy asked Grams for her help and was overjoyed when her grandmother agreed to help her design and decorate the inn.

They continued to talk through their ideas for the renovations, shared thoughts on the overall style and theme of the inn and laughed at how they would definitely need to hire a chef if they wanted truly excellent meals. Grams laughed, "I don't think your guests will appreciate cold cereal for breakfast every day, which is what they'd get if you or I cooked for them." Cassidy grinned. She had to admit that cooking was not her family's strong suit.

Cassidy reached over and gave Grams a big hug and thanked her for agreeing to help with the inn. With the details ironed out, grandmother and granddaughter parted, both excited to get started.

Everything was in place. The renovation permits were done. The contractor was hired. Grams was going to join in the project. Life was good.

But Grams died later that same day. The brilliantly colored Autumn afternoon that started out to be so special quickly became one of the saddest days of Cassidy's life and it felt like the end of her dreams.

Today was the five-year anniversary of Grams' death.

Still staring out the window at the lake Cassidy thought back through everything that had happened. The sad days where she could barely get herself together. The days where everything went wrong and she wanted to give up on her dream. The days when construction issues and delays almost forced her to scream, slam the front door and never look back. But somehow, she survived it all and the inn opened...and so far, her business was turning out to be fairly successful.

Cassidy noticed a brilliant ray of sunlight forcing its way through the trees, making a blinding reflection on the lake. It made her smile. *Hi Grams, I get it—you are reminding me it's time to get moving. Another day to live my life, do good in the world and make you proud. And yes, I'll remember to smile.* Those were the last words her grandmother had said to her five years ago and those were the words she tried to live by every day.

The sound of her friend Trish loudly calling her name startled her out of her trip down memory lane and jolted her back to the present. Cassidy really didn't have time to dwell on the past right now. She could hear the faint sounds of her guests starting to stir upstairs and she needed to get busy. She took one last look out the window at the gorgeous day and quickly walked back to the kitchen to talk with Trish.

Cassidy explained the situation about her chef, Peter, being gone due to his mother's emergency appendectomy.

"Oh no, and at one of your busiest times of the season," Trish frowned, unzipping her black leather jacket and plopping her petite body onto one of the kitchen stools. "Not to mention it's Saturday. When do you think he'll be back? I'm happy to help serve and as usual I assume Amanda will help with the cleaning staff so the new guests can check in this afternoon. But the inn has always been known for its delicious breakfast, and now with your newly renovated dining room offering Sunday Brunch, who will cook these great meals everyone is expecting?"

Cassidy gave her friend one of her famous eye-rolls. "We can worry about Sunday brunch later. Right now, we need to worry about getting breakfast ready today. We only have thirty minutes to whip up a full assortment of breakfast foods so let's get at it."

"I'll do my best, but you know cooking's not my thing."

"Nor mine, but I'm sure we can manage together."

The two women took a deep breath and marched back into the kitchen to gather the various ingredients they needed. Twenty minutes later they were delivering food to the buffet area, filling up the electric warming dishes and then returning to the kitchen for the cold items.

"I expected Amanda to be right behind me. Where do you think our sleepyhead is this morning?" Trish asked.

Cassidy smiled. "I think I saw that fancy foreign car go through town late last night when I was cleaning the porch. I assume she had an extremely late night. I felt bad about sending out the call for help so early this morning, but I can't do it all without the help of my two super-women friends. You are terrific with the guests and the front desk and Amanda has a way of getting 110% out of the staff without ruffling any feathers. I also need to call my mother to see if she can lend me her part-time cook to help out for a few days. We already have a full dining room for Sunday Brunch."

Cassidy and Trish continued to put the finishing touches on the breakfast buffet just as their first guests came into the dining room.

Mr. and Mrs. Connelly were always early risers. They were a lovely couple that first came to the inn over twenty years ago under the prior owner. Over the years as the inn became run-down, the Connellys had to find another place for their annual family vacation. Mr. Connelly once told Cassidy that he and his wife drove by the inn many times while it was being renovated and they were so excited to see the improvements she had made.

When Cassidy opened five years ago her first booking was from Mr. and Mrs. Connelly, and they'd booked with her every spring since then. The elderly couple always took the large two-bedroom suite and the adjoining suite to accommodate their group, which consisted of their married children.

Their oldest son John, and his wife Elizabeth, were expecting their first child, and the senior Connellys were looking forward to meeting their first grandchild. Since the baby was due in a month, Elizabeth was staying close to the inn most days, relaxing, reading and taking short walks along the lake. Elizabeth was strikingly beautiful with a short pixie-style haircut, which set off her large green eyes. Even at eight months pregnant, she carried herself well, except for slightly swollen ankles.

The Connelly's youngest daughter, Isa and her husband Bruce, also came along on the family vacation, but were leaving a few days earlier than the rest of the family so they could visit friends in Portland.

Almost as soon as the sweet gray-haired couple filled their coffee cups and sat down to wait for the rest of their group, Mrs. Connelly caught Cassidy's attention.

The prior day Mrs. Connelly had asked Peter to make a picnic lunch for them to take down to the beach. When she'd heard that the head chef had to leave due to a family emergency, Mrs. Connelly had asked Cassidy for the name of a local restaurant that might be able to supply a picnic-style lunch. Since she always tried hard to please her guests, Cassidy offered to make the picnic lunch for a small fee, and Mrs. Connelly had been delighted.

What was I thinking? Cassidy now scolded herself, her mind reeling. She didn't need something else to add to her long list of things to do this morning. Now she had to rush back into the kitchen, put the final touches on the breakfast buffet *and* pull together the lunch. Cassidy stopped by the storage room and grabbed one of the picnic hampers she collected. Each hamper had a brass plate added to the front that said "Provided to Guests of Crystal Lake Inn. Please enjoy your meal and kindly return the hamper". Cassidy loved that her large collection of antique picnic hampers was being put to good use.

Just as Cassidy was adding the linen tablecloth and napkins to the top of the picnic hamper, Trish came running into the kitchen to grab a refill of scrambled eggs and bacon. It seemed everyone came to breakfast at the same time and everyone was hungry. Cassidy quickly whipped up more scrambled eggs as she put additional bacon in the frying pan while multitasking to add two types of bread to the large industrial toaster.

After getting everything ready to take to the dining room, Cassidy washed her hands and decided to remove her apron since it was stained and changed into one of the newer ones she recently ordered. The aprons had a bib-front with Crystal Lake embroidered on the front and a beautiful picture of the inn with the lake in the background.

The aprons and other customized items were handmade by local artist Sarah Jennings. The aprons became such a favorite among the staff that Cassidy purchased several dozen for her employees. Guests had started to ask if they could buy the aprons for gifts, which gave Cassidy the idea to purchase additional items with the inn's logo printed on them.

She set up the merchandise for sale in the lobby in an old kitchen cabinet her Grams called a Hoosier, which she lovingly restored and painted a bright white with red trim to match the antique canisters she placed on the top for decoration. The display was very eye-catching, and Cassidy was surprised at the large volume of items she sold. As she passed by it now she was reminded that she needed to add another item to her long "to-do" list: restock her display and reorder the fast-moving items.

The last guests were leaving the dining room and Cassidy and Trish were just completing the final clean-up when their friend Amanda came rushing into the room. Amanda was strikingly beautiful with long brown hair and was the tallest of the three women at five-foot-eight inches in her bare feet. Amanda had come back to Lakeview from New York City about a year ago after a falling out with her father. She had explained to her friends that she was tired of playing hostess for her dad's international property management firm and she missed the lake. Amanda seemed a bit adrift, but her friends were happy to have her back, so they didn't pry.

"Well, look who finally decided to come help us. It's about time," Cassidy said.

Amanda was breathless and her face was flushed above her white lace top as she gracefully removed her cashmere cardigan. It was easy to see that her clothes were expensive, yet she had a way about toning down the overall effect by wearing inexpensive sneakers. Not many women could pull off wearing department store sneakers with a Rodeo Drive cashmere cardigan, but Amanda absolutely could.

"I'm so sorry for not being here to help during the breakfast rush. I didn't see your text message until a few minutes ago. I had a late night and couldn't get moving this morning."

Cassidy quickly looked over at Trish, wondering who was going to ask for more details, but Amanda firmly put up a manicured hand like a stop sign. "We can discuss last night later. Right now, we need to get busy. Anyway, I don't kiss-and-tell," she hastily added over her shoulder as she headed upstairs to get the cleaning crew organized. She only got to the second step when she stopped and asked how many new guests were checking in that afternoon.

Cassidy went to the front desk to check the reservations. A family of four was replacing another family just getting ready to check out. When they were this full Cassidy typically saved a room for emergencies and walk-in guests. But these were unusual circumstances. As she was trying to change their online reservation system to 'no vacancy', a reservation request appeared for their largest suite. Cassidy only had a minute to decide whether or not to reject the request, but since it was for only one person, she didn't see the harm in it, so she accepted it. Cassidy told her friends they would have another full house.

Something in the special request comments caught her eye and she stopped to read the entire thing. She knew immediately that she should have rejected the reservation.

"Hey girls, let me share the last-minute booking details with you so you are aware. The information left on the online reservation was a bit interesting. Mr. Burnett, who doesn't provide any other details, says he wants a large suite that's private and quiet. He indicated he only wants maid service when his DO NOT DISTURB sign isn't on his door. He's asked for a three-week rental with the option to extend another month if he's happy with his stay."

Cassidy looked up at her friends, who gazed back at her perplexed. "Don't you think his request is a bit odd for our inn? Most of our guests are here to take advantage of the lake, hiking, sightseeing or day trips to the artisan community up at Pineview Mountain. Our guests don't typically stay in their rooms all day."

The two women shrugged their shoulders, so Cassidy decided not to worry about it and all three went their separate ways. Trish headed to the front desk to check out a few guests and Amanda continued upstairs to help with the cleaning crew. Cassidy went back to the kitchen to make a few phone calls and to review the menu plans for the week. Her chef, Peter, was super organized and planned everything a week or two in advance. She let out a sigh of relief when she saw that many of the breakfast dishes and some of the Sunday Brunch items were already made and stored in the freezer. That would simplify the cooking, a least a little bit.

The next three hours flew by and finally Cassidy, Amanda and Trish met in the kitchen for a late breakfast. They only had the two large suites left to clean, so it was a good time for a break. Cassidy had eggs on the stove, croissants in the oven and was setting the kitchen table when she heard a strange noise and turned to see every light on the control panel of the industrial range and oven blinking. It was almost as if the appliances were yelling at her to do something—*but what?* She had never seen this happen in the past and she didn't know what to do. She stood frozen for a moment and then she noticed that the temperature on the oven was rising quickly. Cassidy yelled, "What the heck is going on? The temperature is rising by itself." She quickly turned off both the appliances, but it was too late. The smell of burnt food assaulted her nose.

Amanda and Trish jumped in to help Cassidy open windows and toss the offending food items into the trash. Cassidy tried to turn the oven back on, flipping switches and turning knobs, but nothing happened. "Oh no," cried Cassidy. "This is a total disaster!" While her friends continued to clean up the mess, she quickly walked down the hall to the office to call the appliance repair shop in town. Luckily, the repairman told Cassidy he would be there in two hours. She crossed her fingers that everything would be working in time to prepare her famous chocolate chip cookies for later that day.

Cassidy firmly shut the door between the dining room and the kitchen to help contain the terrible smell. She continued to try and coax the oven back to life. Amanda and Trish went to the storage room to gather supplies, but they firmly shut the door to prevent the burning smell from spreading across the lobby.

None of them heard the ringing of the bell at the front desk. Not the first time, nor the second, nor the third time it rang. The inn's newest guest was desperately trying to get someone's attention. He didn't know what was going on at Crystal Lake Inn, but he seemed determined to find out.

CHAPTER 2

Jack Burnett was tired, hungry, and just wanted to grab a quick breakfast after his long drive from New York City. After tossing and turning for several hours, Jack had decided at three a.m. he'd had enough debate with himself, so he'd gotten out of bed, showered, thrown his luggage in his car and hit the road for his long drive to Lakeview.

Jack rang the bell again and his frustration was building. He paced, looking around the inn's lobby. He saw a room off to the right and immediately noticed how inviting the place looked. A large picture window made a frame for the shimmering lake and the reflection bounced off the glass front of a large antique bookcase. Walking over to peer inside the case, Jack was surprised to see several rows of the latest best sellers, including his two latest novels. He was impressed with the quality of the mahogany tables and chairs placed around the room and how they were arranged to create smaller conversational areas. It was clear to him that a lot of care had gone into the selection of furniture and how it was placed in the room.

Wandering back to the front desk, Jack still didn't see anyone coming to his aid. A loud rumbling sound from his stomach reminded him that he was starving so he ambled into the dining room hoping to snag a quick breakfast. Just his luck. He only found a few of those small individually sized boxes of cereal and some milk. *At least there's a coffee pod machine.* He decided to pass on the cereal and filled his thermos with hot coffee.

Jack walked back to the front of the inn, and no one had yet come to the front desk. He walked around the living room and library but still couldn't find the innkeeper. At this point Jack's frustration was at a boiling point and his energy was quickly draining. He needed to get to his room and start working. Work was his sole purpose for coming to Crystal Lake Inn.

Jack finally decided he'd had enough, and he dug his phone out of his pocket. Maybe he could try calling the inn. He noticed the inn's business cards on the counter, so he picked one up, located the phone number, and dialed it.

"Thank you for calling Crystal Lake Inn. This is Trish. How can I help you?" he heard a pleasant voice say.

"This is Jack Burnett and I want to check into my room...now!" As Jack launched into a tirade about the lack of service he looked up and saw a petite woman in her mid-thirties with blond hair and blue eyes walking toward the front desk. He immediately noticed that she had a cell phone to her ear. When he realized he was now yelling at the woman standing three feet away from him, he quickly disconnected his call. Now Jack was not only frustrated but also embarrassed.

After an uncomfortable moment, Trish introduced herself and tried to explain why no one had greeted him. "I'm so sorry that no one was at the desk to meet you. We had a little mishap in the kitchen that we were trying to clean up and...."

Jack immediately interrupted her and demanded to be checked into his room. He heard his stomach growl again and watched the young woman try to hide a smile.

"...uh...um..." Trish nervously stuttered. "You see, I'm sorry but your room isn't quite ready yet sir, and the breakfast service is over and...well...." His glare silenced her.

He crossed his arms and sternly frowned. "What kind of inn are you running here?"

Trish apologized again, agreed to check him into his room and gave him the key, indicating that he could come back in two hours and go straight to Room #5.

It was obvious by the scowl on Jack's face that he was still not happy. He stood quietly for a minute, weighing his options. Crystal Lake Inn was the only available reservation within miles when he checked the area yesterday. Realizing he was stuck here for now, he let out a long sigh and asked for directions to a restaurant in town.

Trish politely provided the answers to Jack's questions, and he stomped outside to his car without another word.

Cassidy joined Trish at the front desk and peered out of the lobby window to watch Jack's car drive off, sending gravel flying. "Who was that?" she asked.

Trish frowned. "That was a very, *very* unhappy camper and…." Before she could finish, her phone rang, and she quickly answered.

Cassidy busied herself as Trish walked over to the corner of the lobby and then slumped in one of the winged back chairs, her head bent and her brows furrowed. "Uh huh…okay…I'll be there." Trish stood and quickly walked toward Cassidy, running her hand through her blonde hair, her face scrunched up in worry and her normally bright blue eyes clouded with concern.

"That was Stacy calling." Cassidy knew that it wasn't good news if the manager of Trish's gift shop was calling. "I've got to leave but should be back to help later tonight. Sorry, Cass, I gotta run." Trish gave her friend a quick hug, bolted out of the inn's front door and ran down the steps to her motorcycle. Cassidy forlornly gazed out of the window again, watching Trish throw on her helmet and take off toward town. *Everybody's in a hurry to get out of here this morning,* she mused.

23

But then a bigger worry struck. Cassidy suddenly realized that Trish never told her the name of the unhappy guest. Was it Mr. Burnett who booked Room #5 or was that Mr. Miller, party of four, who booked the family suite? Cassidy quickly rushed to the inn's front door to question Trish, but her words were lost in the roar of the motorcycle.

Cassidy trudged upstairs to help Amanda get the final two rooms ready for check-in. Reaching the second floor, she opened the door to the inn's largest suite and saw the large amount of work still to be done. She regretted accepting that last reservation, but it was too late. She had an uneasy feeling that the guest was going to be a problem. Still, even her worst guests typically didn't force her to evict them. "I guess we'll just have to put up with him," Cassidy muttered to herself.

Two hours later Jack Burnett walked through the lobby and headed straight for the elevator to the second floor. After the embarrassing encounter with the front desk clerk, he wanted to avoid running into her again. He quickly found his room and dropped off his briefcase and suitcase.

After another trip back to his car to get the items he purchased at the small grocery store, including coffee pods and creamer, he piled everything on the mahogany desk that graced the spacious suite. He noticed that the bed was king-size, and it looked comfortable. There wasn't a single wrinkle in the pale blue bedspread and the large pile of pillows was lined up perfectly. Walking into the bathroom to put his toiletries away he noticed the towels were large and looked new. Next, he went to the closet to hang up his clothes and was surprised to see that it was a walk-in. It wasn't huge but it was large enough to not only hang up his clothes but to also store his suitcase and extra shoes. There were framed pictures of the lake hanging on the walls and a vase of fresh tulips sitting on one of the nightstands flanking each side of the bed. It was clear that every effort had been made to help guests feel welcome.

Jack took a second to look out the window and saw the beautiful rolling green lawn, the sun shimmering off the water in the lake, a paved walkway around it with benches dotting the landscape. It seemed like the perfect place to help him overcome his writer's block. *But will it?* Jack wondered pensively.

The tense scene yesterday in his publisher's office still haunted him. Back in New York City, Jack's life was fairly neat and organized. He insisted that his book deals require the minimal amount of book signings and appearances possible. Jack was somewhat of a reclusive author, particularly when working on a book. It took all of his concentration to keep his writing flowing. Too many interruptions and personal appearances while his book was under construction cost him wasted time. The creative flow just seemed to dry up.

After several years of limited success as a writer, Jack was now fortunate enough to be an author with a string of bestsellers. His current project was a three-book deal, and the first two books became immediate *New York Times* bestsellers when they were released. Book three, though, was now months overdue.

Yesterday Jack's publisher delivered the bad news—either get the book done or the deal was off. "No ifs, ands or buts!" his publisher, Thornton Reed, had warned. Thornton was one of the best in the business and he'd been a good friend to Jack, but the normally composed, gentlemanly agent was under tremendous pressure from the top at the Patterson Publishing Company and it was now flowing straight downhill to the author.

"Jack, you need to get rid of the distractions so you can finish your book. Find a quiet place where you can hide away from your recent notoriety and get the book done. You are more than halfway toward completing the first draft. Do us all a favor and finish writing it. It's not worth the legal hassles our lawyers will put you through if you don't. And I've run out of favors with the brass—no more extensions." Jack had paced back and forth across Thornton's office trying to find a way out of this mess. He'd run out of excuses.

After eyeing the fire escape for a moment as if it would magically provide a way out, Jack had finally said, "Ok Thornton, you win. I'll find a place far away from the city and I'll do my best to hit the deadlines. It seems I don't have any choice at this point. Call off the legal hounds."

The sound of children laughing brought Jack back to the present. *So much for peace and quiet.* Jack heard a door slam at the other end of the hall, then suddenly everything was totally still. He released a long breath, one that he hadn't even realized he was holding. With silence came peace and the potential that he could find the words needed to finish the last half of his book.

Jack slightly raised the window where he'd been standing for over ten minutes and took one more look at the lake, which was an amazing bluish green along the edges, but turned to a vivid lighter blue out towards the horizon. A slight breeze blew into the room and Jack could hear the water lapping against the shoreline. The inn was fortunate that Crystal Lake had a small beach with white sand. Once you walked a small distance either east or west, the shore climbed higher as it gradually worked its way up the mountain side. Along the mountain's edges, gigantic rock formations created a barrier between the water and land. The second story gave Jack a better overall view of the lake. It also explained why he saw bright yellow safety barriers in certain areas around the lake. They must be there to prevent people from wandering off the path and getting too close to the edge of the rocky cliff. The paved path along the lake would provide an inviting place for him to do his daily run, Jack mused *As if I'll have time for extended runs*, he sighed.

Jack turned around and walked back across the room to the provisions he left on the desk. He worked for the next ten minutes to put the items away. He set up the coffeemaker to start a cup of coffee, pulled out his laptop and walked back over to the desk. He was a bit surprised to find such a comfortable office chair in his room. Since the inn was more geared toward vacationers and tourists, he thought he'd be sitting in a hard straight-backed chair for hours. The black leather upholstered office chair looked comfortable, like the one he had back home. That was a plus at least.

He sipped his coffee and settled down at the desk, but immediately noticed he needed to adjust the chair to better accommodate his six-foot, two-inch height. Getting the chair to fit better under the desk, he was ready to get started, yet he continued to stare at the blank laptop screen. It seemed to laugh at him. He started to type, then stopped, then hit delete. Jack started to type again, read what he typed and hit delete again. Then he firmly held down the delete button and wiped out the three paragraphs he'd typed.

This total lack of progress went on for several minutes. This wasn't getting him anywhere, so he decided to reread the last couple of chapters he'd written before his case of writer's block froze his brain. Another fifteen minutes passed, and the blank screen continued to stare back at Jack. He kicked off his brown leather loafers, rolled up the sleeves on his white oxford shirt and ran his hands through his thick wavy black hair. Jack decided to review his original concept for the final book in the series and that's when an idea started to form in his mind.

Jack got up from the desk and paced the floor from the desk to the open window and then from the bed to the door of his room. He repeated this pattern several times. Interesting, in sixty steps he could repeat the same pattern. *Jack, you are wasting time*, he said to himself. One more run-through of the idea forming in his mind, and he smiled. Jack quickly walked back to the desk and started typing. His fingers flew over the keyboard. Before he realized it, he'd finished another chapter. Maybe he was on a roll again. *Keep going and don't stop,* he kept telling himself. Let the story unfold. *Keep going.*

By now Cassidy had checked in the last guests of the day, Mr. and Mrs. Miller and their five-year old twin boys, Logan and Mason. By deduction, Cassidy now knew that Mr. Burnett was the unhappy guest Trish mentioned. She felt badly that Mr. Burnett had arrived during the chaos of the late morning, and she had not been able to personally greet him. She gave a sigh of relief that she was able to put Mr. Burnett at the opposite end of the hallway from the Millers. Hopefully, that would provide her solitary male guest with the quiet setting he requested and have enough separation so that the Millers could enjoy themselves without complaints coming from Room #5.

Cassidy put the final touches on the fresh flower arrangement she kept on the entrance hallway table. She loved that she could cut fresh flowers from her own garden and over time she'd improved her decorating and flower arranging skills. Today, the Rudbeckia plants, better known as Black-eyed Susans, were gorgeous, standing about ten inches tall, with bright yellow petals and black centers. She added a few Daffodils along the outer edges of the large vase and a few sprigs from her lilac bush. The smell was heavenly, like walking into a greenhouse. Taking one last look around and making sure that everything was in perfect order, she headed to the kitchen to grab another cup of coffee and put her feet up for a few minutes.

Standing in front of the large farmhouse style kitchen sink, Cassidy was wondering how best to cope with Peter's absence and her thoughts went back to Mr. Burnett and his difficult arrival. She came up with an idea that she hoped would turn things around with this guest. Since he indicated that he planned to spend most of his time in his room working, although Cassidy didn't yet know what type of work Mr. Burnett did for a living, she thought that cooking him an early dinner would be perfect. He wouldn't need to interrupt his work to go into town for something to eat. The repairman had fixed the oven and stovetop and assured Cassidy they had several years of life left in them. Cooking a meal for her guest would also let her test out the equipment to avoid any issues at breakfast the next day.

Although the late spring day kept most of the inn pleasantly cool and breezy, the kitchen didn't fare so well. Cassidy was already feeling the heat by the time she gathered together the ingredients she needed to make her famous seafood casserole. Luckily, shrimp and scallops were in her fresh food delivery that morning. Once she had the casserole in the oven, she pulled together a small salad and grabbed a serving cart from the storage room. Placing a white tablecloth over the tray she also decided to add a small vase with one fresh red rose from her garden. An hour later everything was ready, and it smelled great.

Cassidy took a few seconds to put on a fresh apron, combed her hair and decided to add a bit of blush and lipstick. *Silly me*, Cassidy thought. *Why am I refreshing my makeup just to deliver a meal to a guest?* She chuckled to herself and headed to the service elevator located behind the kitchen.

Cassidy put a bright smile on her face and just as she was ready to knock on the door, she heard the clicking of a keyboard. *Good to know Mr. Burnett is in his room and my efforts aren't wasted. I bet he'll be appreciative.* She knocked three times on the door and waited. No response. *That's odd. I know he's in the room.* She knocked louder and heard a loud and grumpy, "Go away" from the other side of the door.

She slowly inhaled, stuffing down her frustration. As she reached up her hand to knock again, the door cracked open, and a pair of flustered eyes squinted out at her. "Hello Mr. Burnett. I wanted to apologize for the bit of chaos you experienced this morning. I made you a fresh, homemade…" Before she got out her final words Mr.

Burnett slammed the door in her face mumbling under his breath about not being disturbed.

Cassidy stood in the hallway for a few minutes with her delicious meal, feeling like an idiot. She couldn't believe what just happened. She couldn't remember a guest *ever* being so rude.

She stomped indignantly back downstairs and into the kitchen, storing the casserole in the refrigerator. Thinking back on the encounter, Cassidy realized she only got a glimpse of the guest, but there was something about his blue eyes that seemed familiar. She saw enough to know that her grumpy guest was tall, over six feet at least, with dark hair. Again, her mind went back to those large baby blue eyes. Where had she seen them before? She shrugged it off. *No matter. He might be gorgeous...but that didn't make up for his bad behavior.*

CHAPTER 3

Cassidy checked the dining room one more time to be sure her guests had plenty of snacks and refreshments as they returned from their afternoon outings. Everything was well stocked and tidy.

She looked up and saw the Connelly family coming back from their outing and walked over to chat with them about their day. "I'm surprised you're back already. How was your lunch?" The senior Connellys gave her rave reviews on the lunch she'd packed for them, but their son-in-law walked off to check on his wife Elizabeth to make sure she was following doctor's orders and resting with her feet up.

Walking inside from the back deck, Elizabeth walked over to her husband John and wrapped her arm through his, "Cassidy took excellent care of me while you were gone. She put a big fluffy towel on a lounge chair, made sure I had a few bottles of cold water and even put an umbrella over my chair. What more could I ask for? This place is heaven!"

John thanked Cassidy for taking such good care of his very pregnant wife and they headed upstairs to their room for a relaxing afternoon. Cassidy noticed that the senior Mrs. Connelly stayed back for another moment.

"Can I get you something Mrs. Connelly?" Cassidy asked as she walked over to where her guest stood.

"I don't want to seem like I'm overly anxious about Elizabeth, but this is our first grandchild. We debated even taking this trip since she is only a month away from her due date, but her doctor gave her the all-clear and said that some extra relaxation would do both her and John a lot of good. It might be their last relaxing moments for…about eighteen years," Mrs. Connelly laughed. "Any time we're out, if you could check on Elizabeth every so often, we would genuinely appreciate it, if it's not too much to ask."

Cassidy smiled. "Of course, we'll keep an extra watch over Elizabeth. I'll alert my staff not to hover but to be sure to check in on her. It would be our pleasure."

Looking at her watch and thinking about what was next on her daily routine, Cassidy realized she had about an hour to relax before preparing for their nightly drinks and snacks on the front porch. She advertised the nightly event as the "Sit-n-Sip" gathering. She recalled the book one of her guests from the prior week left for her to put on the community room bookshelf. She'd grab it and spend an hour on the back deck reading. Cassidy walked into her private residence at the back of the inn and picked up the book from her nightstand. Just as she flipped the pages open, her phone rang.

Glancing at the phone Cassidy saw that it was her mother and quickly answered. "Hi Mom. Thanks for calling me back. I really hate to ask, but if you could spare your part-time cook for a few days, I could really use her here at the inn. Peter's mother had emergency surgery today and I expect him to be out for a while. Peter just sent me a text that his mother made out fine, but she'll need help at home for a few days."

Katherine Taylor Moore, better known as Kate by her family and friends, responded with a long sigh. "Cassidy, I hope you remember that this is an extremely busy time for your stepfather and me. The annual fundraiser for the

Lakeview Memorial Hospital is in a few weeks and we do a lot of entertaining with some of the biggest donors running up to the final gala. I'd love to say yes but, I'm not sure our cook can take it on. She agreed to stretch her hours for us already and she has a family of her own to care for. I'll ask but I think you should try to find another solution dear."

"I understand Mother and I'll look around for another option. I've been so busy, and we've had a few challenges this week at the inn, including the most infuriating guest in Room #5. Sorry, the gala slipped my mind."

"A problem guest at the inn?" Kate questioned. "That *is* unusual. What seems to be the issue? Is there something I can do to help? You don't think the guest could be a threat of any kind, do you?"

"Oh Mom. Don't let your mind go wild. I shouldn't have even mentioned it. It's nothing I can't handle. You know we often have guests with odd requests. It's nothing more than me trying to be overly friendly to a guest that constantly keeps his DO NOT DISTURB sign on his door. It's not worth talking about right now. We both have more important things going on that need our attention." Cassidy continued. "While we're talking about the gala, do you remember Sarah Jennings? She's the local artist who created the branded merchandise for the inn. I asked her to create special VIP weekend certificates for your raffle. I'll be sure to drop them off in a few days. Sarah is also making us special gift baskets for the VIP rooms. Which reminds me…once she gets the customized baskets back to us, I have to fill them with weekend essentials and snacks…gotta run Mom." Cassidy said her goodbyes to her mother and hung up, already thinking of her long 'to-do list.'

When Kate hung up, her mind was also going in circles. She worried about Cassidy and the pressure her daughter put on herself to personally oversee every detail of the running of the inn. Even though Cassidy had a small staff and her constant sidekicks helping her, she still seemed to double-check every detail. The inn had great reviews, but life was about more than work and great reviews. Kate knew one of the best ways to help Cassidy with balance in her life was to have a good partner.

Kate had tried to fix her eldest daughter up several times with eligible bachelors but after a few dates Cassidy always called it off saying they were too boring, or they had no desire to live in Lakeview permanently, or all they talked about were their messy divorces. The list of excuses went on and on. Kate recommitted herself to finding a perfect match for her stubborn daughter.

Kate felt fortunate that her youngest daughter, Jennifer, was more sensible in terms of her personal life and had married the man of her dreams three years ago. They were now the proud parents of a nine-month-old baby girl named Addie. Her full name was Adelaide Grace Harding after Kate's mother. Grams would have loved little Addie. She was so precious. Addie had big brown eyes like the other Taylor women and a smile that melted the hearts of everyone.

A frown crossed Kate's face as she remembered that Addie would be almost three years old the next time she came to Lakeview. Jennifer's husband had been transferred abroad for two years and it was such a great opportunity that the couple just couldn't turn it down and had moved to Paris, France.

It was a sad and tearful farewell when Addie and Jennifer had stopped over in Lakeview for two weeks before driving into New York City for their long flight overseas.

Kate missed them terribly but knew it was a fantastic opportunity for Jennifer and Addie to explore cities and countries they wouldn't have otherwise had the opportunity to visit.

No more woolgathering for me, Kate thought, trying to put her matchmaking ideas for Cassidy aside. *I have way too many items on my to-do list.* She picked up the long and still growing list laying near the phone on her desk. The next item was to call her friend Thornton Reed at the Patterson Publishing Company. Thornton promised five personally signed books by the bestselling author, Thomas Burnett. She wanted to make sure that Thornton was shipping the books in plenty of time for the gala's auction. Maybe she could talk him into buying tickets for himself and the handsome author. Yes, that would be what she also pushed for—two additional handsome guests for her gala.

"Thornton Reed," the deep distinguished voice answered.

After some pleasantries back and forth, Thornton asked Kate what he could do for her.

"Well Thornton, I wanted to remind you about the signed books for the hospital's charity auction. If possible, I'd like to get them here a day or two early so we can get the auction set up in advance. Would it be possible to ship them by the end of next week?"

"Kate, I ummm, well you see, there's a slight problem. Our hot author is out of town, basically in hiding so that he can finish his next book. I failed to get him to sign the books before he left town. How about if I see what I can do to get them for you. Maybe you can list the auction item generically and if I can't get Thomas Burnett to sign the books, I'll be sure to get books signed by one of the other chart toppers. Will that work?"

Kate was a bit frustrated, but this opened the door to ask for her other favor. "Oh Thornton, I'll forgive you if you'll agree to purchase tickets to join us in person at the gala. I recall that you mentioned your wife was going to be out of the country on business so I think it would solve our little problem about the signed books if you came in person to the gala and you also brought Thomas Burnett!"

"Kate, I can't make that promise. Thomas is under a strict deadline, and I don't even know where he's hiding. Even if I could talk him into it, the travel would take too much time away from his writing, and his deadline is looming. I don't see how that can work."

Kate had met Thornton at a small publishing firm in New York City, where they had both worked right out of college. They became friends immediately and even dated for several months. Everyone thought they would get married, but then Kate met her late husband and that was it for her. She was in love and quickly said goodbye to the lights of New York and moved to Lakeview, Maine. She would always have a special place in her heart for Thornton...and she figured he must feel the same.

Never one to give up easily, especially when it was for her favorite charity, Kate told Thornton that she knew he could make it work. She promised to call him again in a few days to confirm their plans and quickly added, "and any other donation you might like to make would be appreciated, no pressure of course."

"No pressure ever from the famous Kate Taylor Moore, especially when it's for a good cause. I'll see what I can do about the signed books...and I'll be sure to block you from the call list on my cell phone in the meantime," Thornton joked. They spoke for a few more minutes discussing logistics around the gala, hotel reservations and transportation before bidding each other farewell.

Kate had heard through the grapevine that Thomas J. Burnett was very handsome, but she wanted to see for herself if he might be a good match for Cassidy. She decided to search for him on the internet. A long list of links appeared on her screen. Kate clicked on a recent interview by the *Times*. The article confirmed what she had heard; the author was single, in his mid-thirties and wrote intriguing contemporary spy novels. The article also included a picture of Thomas Burnett. He was indeed movie star handsome, in the same category as Matthew McConaughey...with a strong masculine almost rugged face, a thick head of dark wavy brown hair...and big baby blue eyes that seemed to be staring right back at her.

After reading the article and looking at the picture, Kate was more determined than ever that Thornton should bring Mr. Burnett to the gala. She instantly sent a text to Cassidy to save an afternoon for them to go dress shopping later in the week. Kate wanted Cassidy to have a "killer dress" and an appointment at her favorite hair salon. Kate couldn't force Cassidy and the author together, but she could make sure that Cassidy looked her best. Getting her away from the inn for an evening would be a miracle in itself.

Yes, orchestrating the seating chart would force them together. Kate couldn't wait to see what happened. If she had it her way there would be instant fireworks between the two. Or, on the other hand, knowing Cassidy as she did, it might just turn out to be a dud...nothing but her daughter's famous eyerolls and exasperation. Kate was willing to risk the latter...in hopes of at least lighting a few sparklers.

CHAPTER 4

Jack stretched and ran his hands through his already tousled hair. He'd been at the desk in his room at the inn for the best part of two days. He desperately needed a shower and a change in scenery. He closed his laptop and headed toward the bathroom, but his legs were aching, and he knew he needed a long run along the trail at the lake before he got his shower.

He quickly changed into his running gear and headed downstairs, going out one of the side doors so he could avoid running into that pesky housemaid that tried to barge into his room two days ago. He didn't want to delay his run by trying to explain what the "DO NOT DISTURB" sign meant.

Jack walked to the lake's edge and after doing some stretches, he hit the trail. There was nothing better to clear his head than a good five-mile run. He was totally focused on his breathing and his stride, failing to notice the beauty of his surroundings or anyone else enjoying the gorgeous day. After running his typical five miles, he decided to sit down on one of the cement benches along the trail. Suddenly, almost as if the view just appeared, Jack noticed how the sun hitting the water in the lake made it look like ice. The shimmer was mesmerizing.

Jack began to take notice of other people walking along

the trail. Children were playing in a sandbox at the small playground. People were walking their dogs. He heard the sounds of happy people on vacation. It amused him that he hadn't noticed any of this until he sat down and let his mind rest.

Writing spy novels required deep concentration. He needed to leave a carefully crafted trail of evidence with twists and turns in every chapter. Most people failed to realize the amount of preparation and research required to write a good spy novel. Fortunately for Jack, he had done massive amounts of research, character creation and outlining potential story lines before he started the first book of this latest series, so he had all the basics he needed to finish it—everything, that is, except the right frame of mind.

He also kept some of his "spy tools" handy. Having these visual aids helped him when he was developing various scenes. For example, if the killer was left-handed how would he handle handcuffs? How many small compartments did you need in your luggage to sneak poison past the airport security guards? What did the front covers of passports from various countries look like? Could shoelaces be used as rope to dangle over hotel balconies? Answering these types of questions was one reason Jack carried a small collection of "odd items" in his luggage. It also explained why Jack occasionally had to undergo additional scrutiny when flying the friendly skies.

Jack learned many lessons along his journey as a writer. Doing his homework up front for all three books in the series made the actual writing flow much better.

One thing Jack hadn't prepared for was his sudden thrust into the limelight. Jack was typically an outgoing and friendly person, but when he was in the middle of writing, he needed total concentration. The notoriety he received after two straight bestsellers had become a massive distraction. Every time he got into a good flow of writing he was interrupted, which interfered with his focus. Hence, the major reason why he was in Lakeview, hiding at an inn on the outskirts of a small town.

Looking down at his watch Jack realized that he needed to get moving. He started his walk back to the inn, but this time he moved at a comfortable pace, enjoying the beautiful day and the gorgeous views.

Jack was just about to leave the trail area when he saw two small boys climbing on the rocks near the edge of the lake. The boys looked to be five or six years old. They had crawled under the barriers and were getting closer and closer to the edge of the rocks trying to look over at the lake below, but in an area without any safety fencing. He quickly looked around for their parents or other adults who should be calling them to get off the rocks. Not seeing anyone close enough to help, Jack ran at full speed toward them. He was afraid to yell at the boys for fear they would lose their footing and potentially fall into the lake. The water didn't seem to be very deep at that specific spot, but they could get hurt falling off the rocks.

When Jack was close enough to the rocks that he could lunge at the boys if necessary, he stopped and greeted them. "Hello boys. Are you having fun climbing on those rocks? Did you see the sign that said no climbing allowed?" He tried his best to sound friendly and not overbearing or panicked.

One of the boys turned toward Jack and grinned. "We can't read yet so we didn't know we shouldn't climb the rocks."

Jack gently told the boys to turn around and slide back down toward him. When they simply stared back at him with wide eyes, he could see the boys now seemed a bit scared to climb down.

"I'm afraid," one of the boys said.

"I'm here to help you. Just scoot slowly down the rocks and I'll catch you. You'll be fine." Jack forced calm into his voice, belying his racing heart.

When the boys were almost down, he reached out to

help them both to safety. "Where are your parents? Does someone know you are here by the edge of the lake?" Jack asked, trying to remain cool but realizing his voice was a bit shaky.

"Mommy and Daddy told us to stay in the playground area, but we sort of wandered over here to climb on the rocks. We didn't know we were doing anything wrong." The small boys...twins, Jack noticed now...exchanged worried looks and then both started to cry, saying they wanted their mommy and daddy.

Well, isn't this a fine mess I've gotten myself into, Jack thought. He realized people walking the trail were beginning to turn around to see what the commotion was about. He was trying to coax the boys back to the playground when he spotted a young couple running toward the boys.

The twins jumped off the lowest part of the rock and ran to the couple. The young man walked over to Jack and they stood facing each other for a quick second. It seemed the younger man was sizing Jack up. Since the younger man hadn't actually seen the boys near the rock edge, he wasn't sure what had happened. After a few seconds, the younger man reached out an outstretched hand to Jack and introduced himself. "I'm Jim Miller and it looks like you've met our twin boys, Logan and Mason. This is my wife Pam," he continued as a pretty, but exasperated young woman stepped forward. "I can only assume that the boys were doing something they shouldn't have. I hope they didn't cause you too much trouble?"

Jack returned the handshake and breathed a sigh of relief. "Trouble? No trouble at all unless you count my heart beating out of my chest when I saw the boys nearing the edge of the rocks looking down into the lake. I'm glad you showed up. When I tried to get the boys off the rocks and back over to safety, they started crying. I realized I was out of my element."

Mr. and Mrs. Miller had the boys apologize to Jack. Above the loud protests of the twins, each parent picked up one of the boys and they quickly took off toward the inn. The small crowd that had gathered around the scene burst into a round of applause for Jack. He did a quick nod of acknowledgement. Just as quickly as the Millers had moved on, the crowd also started to thin out and everyone went back to whatever they had been doing before the minor crisis occurred. And Jack's breathing and pulse returned to normal.

Finally, back in his room and fresh from his shower, Jack sat back down at his laptop, his wavy hair still damp, and started to work on a rather complex scene in his manuscript. He needed his "tool kit" and grabbed it from his suitcase. He took out the handcuffs and a couple of the fake passports, which were really just made from photocopies, and worked on a scene where his hero was trying to sneak through customs but got arrested and taken into custody. The scene wasn't coming together so Jack hit delete, which lately seemed to be a highly overused key. He tried again for several minutes but realized he was still too wired over the real-life rescue operation of the Miller twins.

Jack closed his laptop and realized he was hungry. His room was a disaster with clothes and towels thrown over the backs of chairs. The kitchenette was littered with empty food wrappers and half full coffee cups. He was torn between getting lunch at the cute little bistro-style restaurant he saw in town the day he arrived or spending the time to straighten his room. His growling stomach won the war. He would straighten up when he returned. In a hurry to get some lunch, Jack hastily put the DO NOT DISTURB sign back on the door but failed to notice that the motion of the doorhandle allowed the paper hanger to slip off and slide back under the door and into his room.

Jack headed down the back steps and out the side door he'd been using to sneak in and out of the inn unnoticed to avoid running into anyone. As he walked outside, he turned around to look behind him and was sure that no one saw him leave the building, hoping again to avoid a run-in with that irritating housekeeper. He set off at a brisk pace toward town.

About two blocks from the inn Jack noticed a young woman sitting on a bench. As he got closer, he noticed she was quietly weeping. He also couldn't help but notice that she was pregnant and seemed quite far along. He wasn't sure what to do, but he knew he couldn't just walk by her and not make sure that she was okay.

Jack slowed his pace and bent over to pretend he needed to retie his shoe. He then asked the young woman if he could sit down and take a break.

The young woman sniffled a bit and looked up. "Yes, of course, please sit down. After a short pause she said, "aren't you a guest at Crystal Lake Inn?"

"Yes, I am. Hi, my name is Jack Burnett. And you are?"

"Hi Mr. Burnett. I'm Elizabeth Connelly. My husband John and his family are staying at the inn. My in-laws stay here every year. This is my first time staying there. Last year my husband and I were on our honeymoon and missed the trip. I insisted we join the family this year, but as you can see I'm not in shape to join them on their outings."

Jack noticed that Elizabeth had stopped crying and he assumed she was physically okay. "Please, call me Jack. This is my first time at the inn as well. It's really beautiful, isn't it? And the walking trails are fantastic. This is more of a working trip for me, not really a vacation, but I'm still enjoying the inn and how close it is to the town, restaurants and of course, the coffee shop."

"Jack, didn't I see you rescue those little boys earlier today?"

"*Rescue* is too strong a word for what I did. I just coaxed them off the rocks until their parents could get to them and deal with the situation. I'm not that comfortable with small children since I don't have any of my own."

Jack noticed that Elizabeth's smile faded, and she looked

sad. Not wanting to intrude on her personal thoughts Jack remained quiet for a while and then said, "I'm sure you and your husband are excited about the upcoming birth of your child. Is this your first?"

"Yes, this is our first. We haven't told our families yet, but we just found out we're having a boy. I think my father-in-law will be so excited. Another future lawyer to add to the family business. When my husband joined the firm, my father-in-law changed the name to Connelly and Son Law Firm. When my sister-in-law Isa joined the firm, the firm's name became problematic. They got together and agreed to change the name to, The Connelly Law Group. My father-in-law has already been talking about potential law schools for our baby. Personally, I just want to get through the next few months.

"I guess it's silly but right now my emotions are all over the place and I was sitting here being a bit weepy worrying about how to keep my child safe. After I saw the commotion down by the lake and the boys so close to the edge of the rocks it made me worry that I might not always be able to protect my children, which made me cry. Of course, I cry at TV commercials these days."

"No need to apologize. To be honest, I also get a bit emotional when it comes to small children...and puppies. If you ever tell anyone I said that I'll deny it. If you're sure you're okay, I'll be on my way. Or I could walk with you back to the inn."

Elizabeth reached over and touched Jack's hand. "Thank you so much for your concern. I'm absolutely fine. I think I'll sit here for a few more minutes and then head back to the inn for my afternoon nap. You've been so kind. Thanks again."

Jack waved goodbye and continued his walk to the cafe. Along the way he wondered if he'd ever be as fortunate as Elizabeth's husband. Waiting on the birth of a child must be the most amazing experience. On the other hand, his relationships so far had left him with nothing but heartache.

The memory of his last relationship floated across his mind. *Jacqueline.* She was a beauty. Tall, with long slender legs, waist-long dark hair and big green eyes. She almost took your breath away, that is, until you got to know her better. She was extremely career-focused, which Jack typically admired in women, but Jacqueline (who insisted that she never be called Jackie, which she said sounded too common) only had one goal in life—to be a runway model. Nothing else mattered to her. Every calorie had to be planned and she was always worried about her public image. They could only dine at the best restaurants and Jack got tired of the endless rounds of socialite parties.

When Jack's books started to become bestsellers, Jacqueline stepped up her constant pushing to go to even more parties and celebrity events until finally Jack had to say, STOP. He started to insist on a few quiet nights at home and after a few weeks Jacqueline said she needed a break from their relationship. Jack figured he'd give her some time to sort out her feelings.

The two continued to send text messages back and forth and still managed to speak on the phone every few days. But that only lasted a few weeks until Jacqueline responded to fewer and fewer messages and then she stopped responding to his calls and texts altogether.

Jack knew something was wrong, so he went to her apartment to speak to her in person. When he arrived, the doorman who knew Jack well from his frequent visits seemed extremely uncomfortable when he asked if Jacqueline was at home. After being told she was not at home, Jack quietly left. As he was standing on the curb waiting for a taxi, he saw a long black limo pull away from the curb. Staring back at him from the backseat passenger window was Jacqueline and another man who had his arms wrapped around her neck.

His breath almost stopped. Jack was totally stunned.

What was going on? Why hadn't he seen this coming? Thinking back over the past few months, Jack now realized that the signs had been there—he had just failed to see them because he hadn't wanted to.

Three weeks later Jack saw a picture of her and a well-known fashion designer at one of the most prestigious fashion house runway shows in the city. The caption said, "Model finds true love on the runway."

At first Jack was hurt. He thought he'd found his soulmate. He'd even been thinking about a long-term relationship, maybe even marriage. Suddenly he realized that what he actually felt was relief. He and Jacqueline hadn't been a good fit for a long time. She loved the glamor and parties while Jack enjoyed a quiet night at home or dinner at a small local restaurant. After all the chaos from his bestseller status in the city, Jack now knew that the bright lights weren't for him. He also realized one other thing for sure—at least until his third book was published, he needed to swear off women. Period. End of story.

His grumbling stomach brought him back to reality. He needed to get something to eat and he could see the little bistro up ahead. As he approached the entrance, he heard the ping of a text message on his phone. It was from his publisher. "Jack, hoping you are in your 'writer's zone' and pumping out the pages. I'll check in with you again soon, Thornton." Jack's good mood quickly dissolved with the reminder of his writer's block and the overdue manuscript.

Deciding that nothing was going to get accomplished until he had a good meal under his belt he went into the bistro and ordered a larger-than-normal lunch of a double cheeseburger, fries and a large chocolate milk shake. Maybe if he fed his stomach, it would help feed his creativity and his writing would start flowing again. But he needed to keep that pesky woman who tried to push a meal on him at the inn away from his door. He needed total concentration and no distractions. Thinking back on the split-second peek he got of her, he realized that her doe-like eyes and beautiful smile could easily be distractions. *Yep, no distractions.* He'd be sure to avoid those big brown eyes at all costs.

CHAPTER 5

Amanda and Trish were just about done helping Cassidy with the daily room cleaning. Cassidy was grateful to have such wonderful friends. What would she do without them? She hoped she never had to find out. Cassidy walked two rooms down to where Amanda and Trish were just coming out of the next to last room on the second floor. "I'll make you two a deal. If you finish Room #5 without me, I'll go down to the kitchen and make us some lunch. Is it a deal?" Cassidy offered.

"If lunch includes a piece of one of those fresh apple pies I saw cooling in the kitchen, then the answer is yes!" both Amanda and Trish responded in unison.

"That DO NOT DISTURB sign has been on the door of Room #5 ever since that guest checked in. I'm surprised to see it's not there now," Amanda exclaimed.

All three women turned around to look at the doorknob and nodded in agreement that it was okay to clean the room since the sign wasn't on the door. "I want to double check with the guest first since he was rather unpleasant the other day when I brought him some food." Cassidy walked over to the door and knocked several times without getting any response. "I didn't see him go out. Did either of you?"

Trish quickly interjected that she had seen Mr. Burnett leave the inn through the side door about fifteen minutes earlier when she was taking out the trash. "By the way Cassidy, you didn't tell us that this elusive guest in Room #5 was also tall, dark and handsome with the most dreamy blue eyes ever. In other words, he is *totally* gorgeous."

Amanda was staring at Cassidy with her mouth hanging open. "Trying to hide that little fact from your best buddies? Were you saving him for yourself?"

Cassidy was amused by their outburst and assured them that the deplorable behavior of Mr. Burnett totally overshadowed his dreamy blue eyes, and she was happy that he decided to spend so much time in his room. She pivoted around on her heels like a solider in a military parade and headed for the elevator.

Trish used her keycard to let them in the room and as soon as the door was opened Amanda let out a huge sigh. "Look at this mess. Dreamy blue eyes or not, he is a *slob*. Let's get at it and get out of here before he gets back."

The two women got to work. Every towel in the bathroom had been used and was thrown in a corner on the floor. The trashcans were all running over, and the kitchenette counter was sticky from spilled coffee. Amanda found it interesting that the guest had stacked all of his empty disposable coffee cups inside each other, resulting in a tower about three feet high. In addition, all four of the custom painted ceramic coffee mugs were sitting in the sink with varying amounts of cold coffee in them. She decided it was better to not count the number of coffee pods sitting in a container next to the coffee machine. Yuk!

Thirty minutes later they were almost done. Only the desk and the mess around it were left to clean. Having strict rules about not snooping into the guest's belongings, Trish tried to dust around the piles of papers on the desk without noticing the details. She picked up a small leather satchel, similar to a man's toiletry bag, to dust under it and it slipped out of her hand. Bending down to retrieve the items that fell under the bag on the floor, she was surprised to see a pair of handcuffs, several passports, a small object that looked like some kind of recording device and what looked like a complex set of maps with several foreign countries circled.

"Amanda, come look at this. I'm not sure what line of work our Mr. Burnett is in, but I don't think he's here on vacation. This looks like he's into something sinister. Are you thinking what I'm thinking?"

"Trish, this may not mean anything. He just carries around some strange stuff in his luggage. Put it all back inside and let's finish up in here. I'm starting to get a bit nervous." Amanda hugged her arms across her body.

The women quickly finished the final touches on the room and let themselves out. They moved on to the housekeeping closet and walked inside to empty their cart and refresh it in preparation for the next day.

Trish turned to open the closet door to exit but stopped so quickly that Amanda almost ran into her back. "Hey, what's up? Why did you stop?" Amanda was in mid-sentence when Trish put her finger over her lips in the sign to be quiet.

They could hear a deep male voice coming from further down the hall. Someone seemed to be on a cell phone. What he was saying kept them from coming out of the closet. The male voice said "Okay, if you don't think that scenario will work, how about we just go ahead and take him out before he gets on the plane, then we won't have to deal with him ever again." A few moments of silence were followed by the deep voice again. "Great, I'll find a way to get rid of him outside the airport and then we'll board the plane and finish the mission." More silence.

Trish and Amanda continued to stand in silence with the door slightly cracked open. They both knew they shouldn't be eavesdropping, but at this point it would look like they had been listening if they came out of the closet now.

The deep male voice started to speak again. "I'm glad you at least like how I got the woman off our trail. That one was so easy. She was beautiful, yet very gullible. She totally bought into everything we told her. Yep, she is now back at her family's villa in Monte Carlo. I think we can write her out at this point."

The man continued, but as he walked further down the hallway it was a bit harder to hear him. "Trish, crack the door a little more. I can barely hear what he's saying," Amanda whispered.

"Shush," Trish whispered back just as the deep voice started to speak again.

"Okay, I get it. I need to wrap it all up in three weeks, but first I need to take care of that gala thing you committed me to do." More silence. The deep voice got so faint the girls had to push the closet door open enough to try and hear the rest of the conversation. The guy had his back to them and they couldn't hear what he was saying, nor could they see his face. He reached in his pocket and pulled out his room key. Before he even stopped at the door, the women looked at each other and whispered. "Where else? Of course. Room #5!"

As soon as the door to Room #5 banged shut, Amanda and Trish ran down the hallway, down the back stairs and into the kitchen. Cassidy took one look at both women and said, "Oh my gosh, what happened? You both look like you've seen a ghost."

Both Amanda and Trish started talking at the same time and Cassidy couldn't understand a word they were saying. "Both of you sit down at the kitchen table and we'll sort this out. Unless the building is on fire, calm down and one of you tell me what this is all about."

Trish, typically being the calmer one, explained what they had seen in Room #5, which in itself, wasn't all that bad, but once she relayed what they had overheard in the hallway, Cassidy now had her mouth hanging wide open. "Are you both sure about what you overheard? You know what I say about eavesdropping—you never hear anything good."

"I think he's a spy and he is getting ready to take someone out," Amanda said with a panicked look in her hazel eyes, drumming her manicured nails on the stainless steel countertop. "What are you going to do? Should we call the police? The FBI? The CIA?"

Cassidy took a moment to gather her thoughts and then started laughing. "You can't be serious. First of all, you only overheard parts of the conversation and secondly, why would a spy be staying at Crystal Lake Inn? You both need to stop reading all of those murder mysteries and watching so many spy movies. The guy could have been talking about a big business deal and taking out the competition." Cassidy continued to shake her head, wiping tears of laughter from her cheeks, and had to sit in a chair to catch her breath.

Her friends looked at her indignantly. "I just remembered something else he said." Trish frowned. "It was a bit vague…about taking care of something at a gala." Do you think he was talking about the *Lakeview* Hospital Gala? The one your mother and stepfather are hosting?"

Suddenly Cassidy stopped laughing. She thought through the conversation her friends had relayed to her, the rude behavior of Mr. Burnett and his preference to not be disturbed. Could the girls be right? Was there something to worry about? *What was she thinking? Of course not!* She scolded herself for being so silly.

Cassidy told her friends that they were just overly tired since they'd been doing double duty the past week helping her at the inn on top of their normal lives. All three of them were putting in extremely long days. Maybe the stress was getting to them. She'd heard stories of how stress could lead people to over exaggerate or to jump to far-fetched conclusions.

"You two need to get out of here, go home and relax. By the way, I'll be fine here tomorrow. I was able to get some extra help from one of the local cleaning agencies and we don't have a full house the next few days. I'll do a lighter breakfast also. Go on, get moving. I can't thank you two enough for all of your help the past few days, but it's clear you are overworked and need a break. I'll see you on Saturday morning at our normal weekly breakfast get-together."

Amanda and Trish didn't look totally convinced but they agreed they were overly tired and they both had put off several of their own responsibilities to help Cassidy. A day or two to play catch-up would be great. They gathered up their purses, gave Cassidy a hug telling her to be sure to call them if she needed their help, grabbed their prepared lunches sitting on the counter, and headed out.

Cassidy watched them leave and replayed in her head the story they shared with her. Over the years she'd been fortunate to only have had a few problem guests and one or two rather eccentric ones. Cassidy thought it was possible that Mr. Burnett had a, let's say, interesting job, but a *spy*? No way. Not at Crystal Lake Inn. Nothing that intriguing *ever* happened in Lakeview. Nope, her friends were mistaken. The inn was quiet and all seemed "normal." End of story.

Or was it?

The conversation with her friends played over and over again in Cassidy's mind and it was interfering with the accounting work she was trying to accomplish in her office later that night. She closed her laptop and sat for a few minutes, sorting through the story once again. While trying to find a reasonable explanation, her mind was just spinning in circles. This wasn't getting her anywhere. Cassidy decided to head upstairs.

Arriving in front of Room #5 Cassidy paused before knocking. She had formulated a plan in her mind while walking up to the second floor. She would see if Mr. Burnett was in his room and if so, she would politely engage him in conversation, checking with him to make sure his room was satisfactory, and the cleaning was done to his liking. She would politely ask if there was anything she could do to make his stay more enjoyable. Speaking to him personally would help her to sort out the situation.

Lifting her hand to knock, she heard voices from inside the room. The deep male voice carried through the door. Looking around to make sure no other guests were in the hall to see her listening, Cassidy moved closer to the door and cupped her hands around her ear.

"As planned, I'll meet you at the local coffee shop tomorrow afternoon at two o'clock. It's called The Perk. We can talk through the details of our plans then." There was silence for a few seconds and Cassidy assumed the person on the other end of the phone was talking. Then the deep male voice continued. "I've agreed to your terms, okay? Leave it at that for now. We can discuss everything in more detail tomorrow. I've got to get back to work. See you then." The room was silent and Cassidy heard the bathroom door close.

Cassidy realized she was still standing with her ear to the door and quickly straightened up. She hadn't really heard anything that made her worried, but she quickly decided that she needed to ditch her plan to confront Mr. Burnett and hurried down the stairs again to the safety of the kitchen.

Time to put Plan B in place. She would make sure she was at The Perk on Main Street the next day at two o'clock. She sent a text to Trish and Amanda inviting them to join her, telling them she wanted to treat them to a late lunch to thank them. Cassidy suddenly had the urge for an extraordinarily strong cup of coffee.

CHAPTER 6

Finding a table in the far corner of the coffee shop, Cassidy casually walked over and scooted a tall potted fern a bit closer to their table. It didn't totally obscure the three of them from sight, but it blocked them from the view of the majority of café style tables at The Perk.

"What in the world are you doing? You've been acting strange ever since we got here. Something is up. Spill it," Amanda demanded.

"Nothing is up. I just wanted to give us a bit of privacy so we won't be disturbed by that busybody Mrs. Lester. That woman spends half her day here so she can overhear conversations and then she spends the other half of the day relaying them to all the other merchants up and down Main Street. I'm not up to dealing with her today." Cassidy took the chair behind the table so that she had a fairly good line of sight to the front door.

The three women sat and talked about the upcoming gala at the hospital, their plans to buy new evening gowns and get their hair done, and wondering if any eligible bachelors would be at the event. They continued to chat for another ten minutes, Cassidy glancing toward the coffee shop's front door every time it opened.

When Cassidy suddenly stopped talking and picked up a menu, opening it in front of her face, the girls knew something was up.

"Okay, what gives?" Amanda asked. "You know that menu by heart and you already ordered your favorite muffin and coffee."

"Nothing is up. I just saw Mrs. Lester head towards the counter and as I said, I'm trying to avoid her." Cassidy put her face back behind the opened menu.

"Look who's here! I can't believe it," said Trish. "It's Mr. Burnett and he's with another man who looks very distinguished, but a little out of place here at The Perk. Now that I can clearly see Mr. Burnett, he's absolutely gorgeous."

Amanda turned to see the two men heading to a table a few yards away, the younger handsome one dressed in khakis and a blue golf shirt, the other older gentleman wearing a tailored suit and tie. "How do you know that man's name?" she whispered.

"I checked him in at the inn a couple of days ago," Trish told her. "He's the guest in Room #5. I forgot that you hadn't seen him yet."

"Shh…keep your voices down and don't stare. I don't want him to see us." Cassidy continued to hide behind the menu. But she couldn't help herself and continued to peek around it. Trish was right. The guest from Room #5 was gorgeous…and there was something about his deep baby blue eyes that felt familiar, yet she still couldn't place where she'd seen them before.

Trish finally realized why they were at The Perk. "Cassidy, how did you know that Mr. Burnett was going to be here today and why are you hiding from him? What happened after we left yesterday that you didn't share with your best friends?"

Cassidy realized that she might as well bring Trish and Amanda up to speed on what she overheard yesterday and why they were at the coffee shop. When she was done with the story, she told them that she wanted to see who Mr. Burnett was meeting today and possibly overhear some of their conversation. Now, all three women were trying to look nonchalant, but they were not doing a good job of it. The coffee shop was busy, as usual, and they could only hear a few words being said since they were sitting two tables behind the two men who were facing the other direction.

After another five minutes Cassidy realized they should just get up and quietly leave before someone would come over to talk to them and mention the inn, which could potentially draw Mr. Burnett's attention toward them. Cassidy didn't think that Mr. Burnett knew who she was, and he had yet to meet Amanda. He might recognize Trish though since she checked him in.

"Let's quietly get up, walk around behind the big fern plant and sneak out the door without drawing any attention to ourselves." Cassidy felt totally stupid for her failed plan. "You two go first and I'll walk out right behind you. Don't stop until you get outside and down the sidewalk a few stores away…."

Trish and Amanda collected their purses, got up and casually walked out the front door. Cassidy was only a few steps behind them when she accidently bumped into the large plant causing it to almost tip over. She reacted quickly and caught the ceramic planter before it crashed to the ground. *That was a close call.*

But, in her hurry to exit she failed to notice Mrs. Lester, the town's court clerk and local gossip, also heading toward the front door. Cassidy bumped into the plump, middle-aged woman causing an unfortunate chain reaction. Startled, Mrs. Lester took a few steps backward, causing her to bump into the table near the front door, which caused two full coffee cups to spill over, in turn causing everyone in the coffee shop to stare at her. Cassidy could feel her cheeks flush hot with embarrassment and she silently wished she were invisible. She quickly apologized to Mrs. Lester.

As if this entire scene wasn't bad enough, when Cassidy went to say she was sorry to the people sitting at the table where the coffee spilled, the first thing she saw were those gorgeous baby blue eyes. She quickly muttered an apology and continued out the door, but not before she heard the companion of Mr. Burnett call him TJ.

Cassidy didn't stop walking until she was two blocks away from the coffee shop. By then, her friends had seen what had happened inside.

"So much for our covert plan to sneak out unnoticed." Cassidy's cheeks were still flaming hot. "How embarrassing was that little scene? Do you think Mr. Burnett noticed who I was?"

"He was so busy trying to grab Mrs. Lester's arm to help steady her and also trying to avoid the hot coffee rolling across the table toward him that I doubt it. I'm not sure he had time to see your face before you ran out of the shop. What a scene that created. You can be sure that within the hour Mrs. Lester will have shared the story with everyone in town," Trish said.

Cassidy knew she had created a mess. "By the way, as I was running out the door I heard Mr. Burnett's companion call him TJ. The 'J' could stand for Joseph or John, but now we have one more piece of confusing evidence. This is all so strange. I'm not sure what to make of this situation. My instincts tell me it's not what we are building it up to be, but on the other hand, I'm responsible for the inn, our guests and our staff, which for a few more days, includes the two of you. I need to get back to my office and think through everything. I'll call you later."

Returning to her office at the inn Cassidy went back to work on the pile of paperwork on her desk. She also needed to place several food orders so Peter didn't return to a bare cupboard. She was interrupted by the ringing of her cell. Looking down she saw it was Peter.

"Hey Cassidy, did I catch you at a bad time?" her head chef asked.

"No. Now is perfect. I'm in my office trying to whittle down the pile of papers threatening to spill onto the floor.

How is your mother? I hope she's on the mend. I know how active she usually is and how she was looking forward to coming to the inn to visit for a few weeks."

"All is good with her recovery. We met with her doctor yesterday and he told us that she's healing nicely and can start back with some light activity, taking the stairs and walking, but she can't drive for another week. I really hate to ask but would it be possible for me to stay another few days with my mother? My sister's husband will be back from his business trip soon and then she can come stay with Mom. I just want to make sure that everything goes smoothly."

"Okay, I understand." Cassidy sighed.

"How are you coping with everything going on at the inn?" Peter asked. "You would let me know if you were in a real bind there, wouldn't you?"

"You know me, I'm Superwoman and can handle everything. All kidding aside, it's been a bit hectic but with Amanda and Trish helping out and with extra cleaning help I hired, we're keeping our heads above water. I'm a bit concerned about the brunch on Sunday though. We're sold out." Cassidy didn't want to worry Peter, but she also wanted him to know how much she appreciated him and missed him when he wasn't around.

People sometimes teased the two of them that they should be a couple, but honestly, they were more like brother and sister, and she planned to keep it that way. Besides, even though he was good-looking in a surfer-type way with his lithe frame, wavy blonde hair and sea-blue eyes, he just wasn't Cassidy's type. She just didn't know what her type actually *was*. "I do miss you though. But I guess a few more days won't kill me," she teased, trying to keep it light.

"Did you check with your mother about her cook helping?" Peter offered.

"Did you forget about the upcoming gala and all the dinner parties my mother and her husband Duncan host leading up to the event?"

"It seems I picked a really bad time to be away. I'll tell my mom we need to plan her next little emergency at a less hectic time," Peter quipped back.

"No worries. I've handled it before and all of the work you did to plan ahead has been a lifesaver. The girls are coming over tomorrow for our normal Saturday brunch and we plan to do some of the prep work and get the dining room set up for Sunday. I'm so glad that we agreed to wait until after the gala to expand our dining room hours. That will give you time to find an assistant and additional wait staff."

"Hang in there, girl," Peter quickly added before they hung up.

After Cassidy hung up, she looked back at the stack of paperwork and frowned. Glancing at her watch she decided to go to the kitchen and get her cookies started for the Sit-n-Sip. Even though the oven was working fine, she still wanted to keep an eye on it.

An hour later, the cookies were on a serving tray, the drink bar was stocked, and the coffee setup was done. Cassidy rolled the two big carts out to the front porch, which signified to her guests that Sit-n-Sip was officially open for their enjoyment.

A few guests at a time typically joined her on the front porch. Some gathered together in small groups and stayed the entire hour, while others grabbed their refreshments and walked toward the lake.

This was one of Cassidy's favorite times of the day. She enjoyed getting to know her guests and hearing about their adventures and plans for the next day. It was one of the events at the inn that always received high marks on her surveys and online feedback.

The Miller twins ran over to her cart and stared at the cookie tray. Cassidy looked over at Mrs. Miller to get her approval and got a smile and a raised pointer finger.

"Ok boys, your mother said you can have one cookie each. You don't want to ruin your dinner. Have you been having fun the past few days?" Cassidy asked. Both boys vigorously nodded and reached for the largest cookie they could find on the tray. *They're so darned cute,* she thought a little wistfully. *Maybe one day…*

Their mother walked over to tell the boys to find a chair next to their father while they finished their treat. "Cassidy, we love your inn, and the town is just so charming. We've been so busy every day that the boys fall asleep early, which gives my husband and I a little bit of quiet time each evening. Before we leave, I want to book again for next year so we get the same week if possible."

"That would be wonderful Mrs. Miller and we'd love to have you back. I'll be sure to get the dates for next year in our reservation system. I know you plan to leave on Monday to continue on your journey to see your parents. I hope that you plan to join us for our Sunday Brunch tomorrow. Will I see you all there?" Cassidy liked the Millers and was glad to hear they were enjoying their stay at the inn.

Mrs. Miller confirmed they'd be at Sunday Brunch. As she turned to go she stopped and said, "I never got the chance to personally thank the guest that was kind enough to get the boys off the rocks down by the lake a few days ago. We were getting ready to go into town and the boys were right next to us one minute, and then I looked down and they were gone. I had that awful moment of panic when we didn't see them on the lawn or the walkway. As I looked further down at the lake I saw a commotion and I feared one of the boys was hurt, or worse. We took off running toward the crowd in time to see a man helping to get the boys off the rocks. He left so quickly we didn't get his name. One of the onlookers told us that the man was very patient with the boys and slowly coaxed them off the rocks so they wouldn't get hurt. Do you happen to know who it was so I could properly thank him?"

Cassidy shook her head, "I hadn't heard any of this. I'm

surprised no one mentioned it to me. I'm so glad the boys were okay. No, I don't know who that would have been. I'll ask around, though. Are you sure he's a guest at the inn?"

"Yes, one of the other guests, I think her name is Isa, said she'd been sitting on the porch reading and heard the commotion. Later someone told her the man was a guest at the inn but didn't know his name."

"That would be Mr. and Mrs. Connelly's daughter...hmm...let me ask around and see if I can find out who the man was and I'll get back to you. Enjoy your evening and I'll see you tomorrow at brunch." Cassidy walked over to talk to a few other guests but didn't see Isa to question her about the mystery guest who had rescued the boys.

When the Sit-n-Sip was over, Cassidy pulled the carts back inside and cleaned up the leftovers. As she headed to the kitchen, she munched on the last cookie left on the plate. There were only a few dirty dishes so she filled the sink with hot sudsy water, washed, dried and put the dishes away. She was a creature of habit, so she wiped down all the counters before turning out the lights.

Cassidy walked down the hallway to do a last restock of the dining room. She added a few more apples to the large handwoven basket sitting on the oval mahogany table in the center of the room. She also added a few more bottles of water and juice to the beverage fridge that sat along the opposite side of the room. Taking a dusting rag from one of the drawers in the hutch, she carefully wiped down the furniture and turned on a small tiffany-style lamp that she left on all night so that guests could easily get snacks anytime they wanted. Standing back and looking around the room she felt a sense of pride in how inviting the room looked.

Turning around and heading towards the lobby, Cassidy glanced over to the community room and saw Isa Connelly putting a book back on the shelf. She noticed how pretty the young woman was and even though Isa didn't look to be over twenty years old, she knew from the senior Mrs.

Connelly that Isa had already graduated from law school and had joined the family firm last year. Isa carried herself in a confident way, with her head held high. She had great posture and her movements were deliberate, yet graceful. Her body language made you feel comfortable seeking her help, which seemed perfect for someone in the field of law.

"Isa, do you have a minute? I wanted to ask you about what happened with the twins yesterday. Mrs. Miller said you mentioned that you thought the man that helped the boys off the cliff yesterday was a guest at the inn. I hadn't even heard about the situation until this morning so I couldn't help her. Do you happen to know the name of the guest?"

"No, I don't know his name. I only saw him one time. We passed each other in the upstairs hallway. He never comes to breakfast or the Sit-n-Sip so I don't know his name, but he was so kind and gentle with the twins that I thought what a nice man he must be. That's what made me notice him this afternoon when he returned to the inn. I saw him go into his room."

"Do you know which room it was? Then I can match up his name from his room registration."

"Yes, it was Room #5," Isa said as she picked up another book from the shelf and walked back toward the stairs to the second floor.

It couldn't be Mr. Burnett, Cassidy thought. *How could a nasty person like that be so kind to the boys and go out of his way to keep them from getting hurt?* Isa must have been mistaken.

Cassidy would just have to keep asking around to find out who really should get the credit for saving the twins. Nope. No way was it Mr. Grumpy, err…Mr. Burnett.

CHAPTER 7

"I'm so glad you two came over yesterday to do some brunch prep work. This morning is going smoothly so far, but I won't relax until the last guest leaves the dining room. We get such great reviews on our Sunday Brunch and Peter has worked so hard for those reviews. If I mess it up today, I'll have to post an apology saying that it was my fault."

Clearing off the last remnants of French Toast and Eggs Benedict from the large table by the window, Cassidy took a minute to say goodbye to a few guests that were checking out that morning. As she walked over to the front door that led to the porch to help the guests with their luggage, she noticed Sarah Jennings, the local artist that supplied the hand-painted items for the inn, coming up the long, winding walkway. She had several big boxes in her arms.

"Here, let me help you with those," Cassidy said as she rushed down the front steps of the inn.

"You are a life saver Cassidy. My arms were starting to give. I should have made two trips. I was so excited to show you how well everything for the VIP event turned out." Even though she was young and in shape, Sarah was breathless.

Once inside the lobby, Cassidy said, "let's take these into the office. I can't wait to see what you've done. Your work is always so beautiful. I'll get a cart out of the closet to put these boxes on and make it easier for both of us."

Cassidy pushed the cart down the hall that led from the front of the inn to the area behind the kitchen. The office had a long and well-worn table they used for a variety of things like sorting inventory, staff meetings and sometimes an overflow of delivery items. The two women took the boxes from the cart and sat them on the long table. Sarah opened the first box and pulled out five beautifully framed VIP Weekend Vouchers. Each one was handwritten in script with a hand-painted view of the inn and the lake.

Cassidy admired her inn from the artist's point of view and her eyes welled up with tears. The artist had painted the lovely two-story clapboard building with its many windows and big wraparound porch dotted by white rockers across the entire front of the inn. This was offset by the sweeping green lawn and shimmering blue water of the lake in the foreground framed by cattails and wildflowers. It captured the relaxing and gracious essence of Crystal Lake Inn. "These are gorgeous Sarah. My mother is going to love them."

Sarah then opened the second box and pulled out one of the handwoven baskets. Each one had a brass plaque on the front, a cloth liner inside and a handle made of leather. The plaque said: Crystal Lake Inn—VIP Gift Basket.

"The remainder of the baskets will be delivered by our deliveryman mid-week, but I wanted to make sure you were happy with these before the weavers make the rest of them. What do you think?"

Cassidy did not immediately reply, struck speechless at first by the quality and beauty of the craftsmanship. Each basket was the same size and shape, yet each one had a different color liner. Some were florals, while others were solid colors, mainly in tans or bright whites.

"I can't wait to fill them with all the inn-branded essentials and snacks. They're perfect, thank you!" Cassidy reached over and gave Sarah a big hug. "Sarah, you help to make our inn look good. All the special touches get so many comments in our online reviews and you're a big part of our success."

After repacking the boxes and moving them to the storage area, Cassidy walked Sarah back outside. They stood on the sidewalk admiring the beautiful blue sky and maple and pine trees in all of their various bright spring shades of green, then Sarah got in her van with its big logo, Lakeview Artisans, emblazoned on the side and left.

Cassidy glumly headed back to the dining room, where she knew work was still left to be done. It was tough to work inside on such a gorgeous day as this, and she longed to be able to take a walk around the lake like most of her guests were probably doing right now. *There will be time…*she reminded herself. *Someday…when I'm not so busy.*

She walked into the dining room and looked at the chaos, for a moment wanting to escape back outside and run to the lake. Crumbs littered the dark hardwood floors. The cream-colored linen tablecloths and matching napkins were crumpled and stained with various shades of jams, tea and coffee, and the chafing dishes on the buffet table were caked with leftover eggs, meats and hardening toast. *Still, mission accomplished,* she thought with satisfaction.

"Phew," she said with pure relief as Amanda walked into the room, her long hair pulled back in a ponytail, sweat glistening on her pretty young face. Cassidy high-fived her friend, then the two women stood hands on hips in their grimy white coats and black work pants, surveying the aftermath of a brunch that had served forty people.

"It looks like we did it. Everyone's been fed and no major catastrophes. Now we can get everything cleaned up. I'm glad I decided to keep the extra cleaning service for a few more days. You and Trish can go back to your normal lives."

"I'm not really busy right now anyway," Amanda said. "Trish said she needed to put a few hours of work in at her gift shop this afternoon, so I know she'll be glad to get going soon." Amanda walked around the dining room and removed the tablecloths and other linens. "I'll at least get these into the washer before I leave. I think the only thing left is to vacuum the room. Are you sure you're okay to do that?"

"Of course. Now get going and try to enjoy the rest of the day."

Cassidy headed to the closet, pulled out the vacuum and headed back to the dining room. Quickly running the vacuum and straightening a few chairs, she looked around the room. Everything seemed to be in order. Instead of walking across the room to unplug the vacuum, Cassidy did what her mother always told her not to do, she just yanked the cord out of the wall socket. As she yanked it, the cord got taut and raised off the floor a few inches. As luck would have it, at the same time a man walked into the room and immediately tripped over the cord. Luckily, he caught himself from falling all the way to the floor by grabbing a table.

"I'm so sorry!" she said as she walked over to the man. She recovered from the momentary shock of watching someone almost fall thanks to her carelessness only to realize that it was Mr. Burnett, the infamous guest in Room #5. *Of course, it would be him.* Cassidy felt her cheeks burning and was at a loss for words.

Mr. Burnett had dropped his notebook during the fall and Cassidy bent to pick it up. Unfortunately, Mr. Burnett took the same action at the same time and they banged heads. Now both of them were shocked and their hands flew up to their foreheads.

Cassidy tensed up, waiting for the outburst she knew was coming based on past experience. Instead of saying anything else, she waited for Mr. Grumpy to start yelling at her. He seemed to be trying to decide what to say. He didn't speak for what seemed like minutes, although in reality it was only a few seconds. Cassidy noticed he took a deep breath. *Okay, here it comes,* she thought.

But Cassidy was thrown totally off guard when Mr. Burnett started to laugh. Now she was concerned that maybe he was losing it. She didn't know what to do so she just stood there to see what he did next.

She was surprised when he put out his hand and said, "I think we need to start over again. Hello, I'm Jack Burnett. I'm your reclusive guest in Room #5. We seemed to have gotten off on the wrong foot and I wanted to apologize for my behavior the day you tried to show me some kindness and you brought food to my room. I was a bit grumpy that day."

Cassidy was stunned. Instead of saying anything she just continued to stare at him. His hand was still thrust out toward her. She noticed his white shirtsleeves were rolled up, revealing strong forearms that matched the rest of his tall, dark and handsome frame. She quickly noticed his shirt was tucked into dark blue jeans with a brown leather belt around his waist. And of course, she couldn't help but notice his big baby blue eyes. WOW, they were gorgeous!

She finally pulled herself together and reached out to return the handshake. "Hello, I'm Cassidy. I know better than to yank a cord across a room. Since brunch was over I didn't expect anyone to come in, but I should know better. Are you okay Mr. Burnett?"

"Please call me Jack and yes, I'm perfectly fine, well, except for a red spot that's probably on my temple. You seem to have a matching spot on yours. Maybe it's a new fad." Jack gave her a boyish grin, his charming blue eyes sparkling. "I came in here to grab something to eat, but I always seem to be a little too late. I'll just grab some fruit if that's alright. It was nice finally getting to meet you and getting the opportunity to apologize for my behavior." Jack walked over to the bowl of fruit and picked a big red apple and started to walk out of the room.

It suddenly hit Cassidy that Jack didn't know that she owned the inn. She looked down at her grubby work clothes. He probably assumed she was one of the housekeepers or cooks. It seemed like a good time to explain who she was and get to know him better. She could also sneak in questions about what he was doing in Lakeview.

"Wait…please. If you give me five minutes I can get you a plate of hot eggs and bacon from the warmer in the kitchen. What type of toast would you like?"

He turned, his tall frame filling the doorway. "That's too much trouble Cassidy, but I do appreciate the offer."

"No trouble at all. I really want to make it up to you for the chaos of the day you checked in and the little mishap just now. Please let me fix you a plate." Cassidy knew she sounded like she was pleading but this was her opportunity to put some of her fears about Jack to rest—or confirm she had a big problem on her hands.

"Okay. On one condition…if it wouldn't get you into any trouble, would you join me? Is it a deal?" asked Jack.

Cassidy was relieved. "Yes, it's a deal. Help yourself to coffee and I'll be back in a few minutes. And I'm positive I won't get in trouble." She grinned to herself as she left the dining room.

Quickly walking into the kitchen Cassidy looked around for her friends but they had already left. She put bread in the toaster, warmed up a plate of scrambled eggs and bacon, and pulled a tray out to organize the meal. Last minute she whipped off her grimy chef's jacket. At least she had worn a nice pink blouse underneath. She grabbed some pink lip gloss from her purse and applied it and in minutes was walking back into the dining room to sit the tray in front of Jack with a smile.

Jack looked at her, a flicker of…was that appreciation, or more…in his eyes…and smiled back at her.

He took a few bites and stopped to say how delicious the meal was. "I also wanted to thank you for cleaning my room two days ago, but I thought I had left the DO NOT DISTURB sign on the door. I was surprised to see it had been cleaned. It looked so much better when I returned, and your cleaning crew didn't disturb anything. It's not always like that in hotels, so thank you."

Cassidy hoped her flushed cheeks didn't give her away. "I guess the door hanger might have fallen off the door. Sometimes they do that when the door closes. I was with the cleaners and personally saw that the sign was not on the door. I'm glad it all worked out."

"I wasn't complaining," Jack continued. "I was trying to compliment your cleaning crew but apparently I'm not doing a particularly good job of it." Changing topics, Jack said, "By the way, were you at The Perk on Friday? I thought I saw you rushing out the door. I wasn't exactly sure what happened, but when I looked up, I saw an older woman almost falling and hot coffee rushing across the table toward me. I tried to steady the woman and move away from the table at the same time. When I looked again, you were gone. Was that you?"

Not knowing how to get out of this one, Cassidy decided to be honest...to a point. "Yes, my two friends and I often go to The Perk. As I was leaving, Mrs. Lester and I slightly collided and she bumped your table. I was, um, running late to get back to the inn and once I knew Mrs. Lester was fine, I kept going."

To her relief, Jack didn't seem to think that Cassidy's behavior was strange enough to ask more about it and he moved on to talk about how much he was enjoying his stay, getting lots of work done and finding it convenient to be so close to the town, yet far enough away to be able to have some quiet time to work.

"What type of work do you do?" Cassidy asked Jack.

He seemed to hesitate for a second and then said, "I'm working on a project that is overdue and my boss in New York is not happy with me. He sent me away to somewhere quiet so I could concentrate and finish it." *Hmmm, he didn't really answer my question*, she realized.

He went on to ask her, "How long have you worked at the inn?"

Now it was Cassidy's opportunity to come clean.

"I think there is a bit of confusion. I actually own the

inn."

She watched his eyebrows raise and his blue eyes widen in surprise.

"Like many small businesses, it's a hands-on job. We've been a little short-staffed with our chef out on a family emergency. Along with two of my friends and some extra help from a local cleaning service we've been doing a bit of everything around here lately." Cassidy felt much better being totally honest with Jack.

Now it was his turn to blush. "Oh! I guess you don't need the boss's approval to sit here with me since you *are* the boss. Thanks for clearing that up for me. How long have you owned the inn?"

"Five years."

"How did it all come about? You seem too young to own your own inn. I would love to hear about it."

Cassidy relaxed. This was a story she enjoyed telling. She spent the next fifteen minutes talking about how she came to own the inn. She shared how her maternal grandmother helped care for her and her sister when their father died. How Grams, a local businesswoman who had a flair for decorating, had planned to help Cassidy renovate and decorate the inn but died and never got the opportunity. Before Cassidy got teary eyed as she often did when speaking about Grams, she quickly shared a couple of funny stories about her best friends and how her mother, Kate, was always trying to play matchmaker for her. She even managed to mention how her chef's absence added to the confusion on the day Jack arrived.

"Your Grams reminds me of my grandmother," Jack said softly, a faraway look in his eyes. "She was also incredibly special to me. I'm sure you miss her."

"Yes, I miss Grams every day. Her name was Adelaide, but after her grandchildren came along everyone seemed to call her Grams. My niece is named after her."

Cassidy was touched by the way Jack spoke about his grandmother. Not many men would be that open about their feelings. She felt like a tiny hole was opening in Jack's gruff exterior.

"I think that you were the person who saved the Miller twins from getting hurt earlier this week and then I heard about a guest from the inn who stopped to speak with an emotional pregnant woman on a bench near town. It seems this mysterious guest keeps popping up at just the right time. Was it you?"

Jack sat quietly for a minute and then a bright smile appeared on his face and like magic, those baby blue eyes lit up like electric lights. "I'm not one to rescue and tell. Anyone would have done the same thing. Maybe I'm your hero and maybe I'm not," he teased.

If it was him, he was being way too modest not to confirm it for her, she thought. Cassidy was almost startled to realize that maybe she had the wrong impression of Jack Burnett after all. Yet, she was still wary due to what her friends heard in their eavesdropping episode. So, she continued to ask questions and try to uncover more about him. Maybe a few more facts would explain his unusual behavior.

"You mentioned your boss was in New York. Do you spend much time in the city?"

"Yes, but I also travel a lot. This latest project needed some special focus so here I am. Your latest guest, who seems to always be late for breakfast. Let me apologize again for being so rude the day I checked in. You tried to make amends to me. I'm a bit embarrassed by my behavior."

A little more of the gruffness was falling away, and just as Cassidy was starting to get more comfortable with him, he interrupted her thoughts and said something that felt like it came totally out of the blue.

"You're different than most women I know back in New York," he said abruptly, almost like he spoke without thinking.

Cassidy waited for him to continue but he was intently looking at her. At first she was taken aback. Was he looking down at her? She assumed he was used to smartly dressed women in business suits and heels. Should she be insulted?

"Let me explain. I meant that in a good way. You are easy to talk to and it's clear that you take great pride in the inn. It must be hard work, yet you always have a big smile on your face, and I see how hard you try to make your guests feel at home." His baby blue eyes twinkled, and a slight blush creeped up his neck to his cheeks.

Cassidy felt like she was a yoyo on a string. She went from feeling good about Jack to feeling insulted, and then he said something so nice it made her smile. She saw a look in his eyes that said he wanted to get to know her better.

Just as Cassidy was about to ask another question, Jack's phone rang.

"I'm sorry to interrupt our conversation but this is a business call and I have to take it." Jack suddenly lost the smile and was all business again.

She felt dismissed. The charm was gone, and he was all business. *Flip-flop.* As Cassidy got up from the table, she overheard him saying something about 'taking care of business and telling the caller to stop pestering him—he'd get the job done'.

Cassidy noticed some guests at the front desk and went to see if she could help them. Yet, her mind kept wandering back to the confusing conversation with Jack. As much as she wanted to ask him a few more questions, she finally felt comfortable that he wasn't a threat to the inn. But on the other hand, something about him left her unsettled. She felt like he was hiding something and that made her nervous.

She also felt a slight tug at her heartstrings. That was odd. In a thirty-minute conversation could you really go from believing someone was a rude and grumpy person to thinking he was someone you might want to get to know better? Why was her heart racing? Why did she keep looking into the dining room to steal a look at Jack? She suddenly realized that what she was feeling was attraction and right now, she didn't have any room in her life for getting involved. Besides, she had a strict rule about not dating guests.

Cassidy decided right then that the best path forward was to avoid running into Jack as much as possible. He only had a week left of his reservation. She could find creative ways to avoid him if she tried hard enough.

A few hours later Trish and Amanda stopped by to join her at Sit-n-Sip. After ensuring her guests were well taken care of, the three friends moved down to the end of the porch. Cassidy caught them up on what she called the "Vacuum Cleaner Incident" and her head-butting with Jack.

"So, what do you think now that you've had the chance to have a meal with him? Is he a spy?" Amanda asked.

"Shh, keep your voice down. I don't want anyone overhearing us. No, I truly don't think so. One of the guests told me about a guest from the inn saving the Miller twins from getting hurt on the rocky cliffs by the lake. She said he was very patient with them and coaxed them down slowly so they wouldn't get hurt. He didn't even stick around to get any accolades for doing a good deed. I asked him about it, but he wouldn't confirm or deny it. I don't know if it really was him, but the guest that mentioned it to me said she saw him go into Room #5. Doesn't it seem like all roads leads to Room #5 lately?" Cassidy seemed to go into deep thought about something, but realized the girls were looking at her, waiting for more details of her meeting with Mr. Burnett.

"I think there must be some simple explanation for what we overheard. Keep in mind that we only heard bits and pieces of several disjointed conversations. For all we know, he could be a private investigator, or he could be in police work and he's here working on some type of research paper. Or he could be a thousand other things. It's really none of our business." Losing her train of thought, Cassidy continued, "but those baby blue eyes. I know I've seen them somewhere before. A girl could get lost in the depths of those eyes."

Realizing she said the last bit out loud she stopped and looked at her friends, both of whom were staring at her with big smiles on their faces.

Trish was the first to speak. "We knew it. That's the second or third time you mentioned his baby blues. When was the last time you took an entire half hour to sit down and eat with a guest? You are interested in Mr. Burnett, aren't you?"

"No way. You both have also mentioned his blue eyes. I just wanted to show you another side of Mr. Burnett so you'd stop trying to make him out to be some type of international spy."

Eager to change the subject, Cassidy continued, "My mother reminded me yesterday that I put off dress shopping with her for so long that we didn't have time to go to New York City as originally planned. I'm sure we can find something fabulous at the new designer dress shop in town. Are you both available to go shopping on Tuesday afternoon? I have someone who can cover the front desk and take care of things here at the inn for about four hours. That's enough time to slip into town, do our shopping and maybe grab a coffee at The Perk."

Both Trish and Amanda confirmed they were available and a few minutes later they left the inn. Cassidy tidied up the porch, cleaned up the kitchen and headed to her room.

Once there, Cassidy spent a few minutes going through her personal emails and checking the inn's email account. She also checked on reservations for the following week and month. She was glad to see that reservations continued to be high.

Deciding to take a look at the night of the gala, she saw the inn only had a few rooms left. Cassidy wanted to enjoy her evening at the big event so she had blocked out most of her rooms almost a year ago when the gala's date was first confirmed. This was one evening she and her friends were going to thoroughly enjoy. The annual Lakeview Hospital Gala was the biggest party in town and it was for such a great cause. Her mother and stepfather were so good at gathering donations, with each year's total exceeding the prior one. She was glad to be there to enjoy the evening with family and friends and also to support her mother's favorite charity to benefit a new Neonatal Unit.

What she didn't look forward to was her mother trying to set her up with a date. Every year her mom tried to arrange for an available bachelor to sit next to Cassidy at dinner. And every year Cassidy was able to either rearrange the name cards before her seating partner sat down or she swapped seats with someone else. It had become a game between her and her mother—one Cassidy was getting tired of playing. She needed to have an open and honest discussion with her mother on this topic again. Not that it would do any good.

It was getting late. As she typically did, Cassidy wanted to check that the dining room snack area was full before the front door automatically locked at eleven o'clock. Guests could use their room keys to come and go, but the door stayed locked until six the next morning. If someone without a key needed to get in, they could press a buzzer, which would notify Cassidy's and Peter's cell phones. This seldom happened unless guests were delayed checking in, but typically in that situation, someone would call her directly. If they weren't too late, she sat in the community room and read until they arrived so she could personally greet them.

Everything was in order in the dining room and the community room was empty. She turned off most of the extra lights, being sure to leave on a few so there was a clear pathway down the stairs, through to the dining room and the community room.

Just as Cassidy started to walk back to her room, she

heard a child crying on the second floor. It was a faint sound. She guessed one of the Miller twins didn't want to go to bed. She waited a few minutes and the crying stopped so she headed down the hallway to her private residence.

It seemed like it was going to be a quiet night at the inn, which was just what she needed, especially after the stress of Peter being away and her two encounters with Jack.

Yes. Peace and quiet. That is exactly what Cassidy needed.

Once in her room Cassidy quickly got into comfy clothes and the fluffy slippers Trish had given her the prior Christmas. The slippers had puppy dogs with floppy ears on the toes of the shoes. She thought they were absolutely adorable. Cassidy kept thinking back to her breakfast with Jack. It wasn't really a breakfast; it was more of an apology for almost tripping him with her vacuum. Who knew a vacuum could be a deadly weapon? She needed to be much more careful about how she used her cleaning tools in the future.

Herbal tea always helped her to relax so she quickly made a cup and propped herself up on several pillows in bed. She still hadn't had time to start the new book the guest had left behind for her. Tonight was the night to start the book and take her mind off of everything else.

She reached for the book on the nightstand but, just as had happened a few days earlier, she hadn't even opened it when she heard kids crying again, only this time louder.

CHAPTER 8

The commotion of children wailing was coming from the lobby. Knowing that it was best to go to the front desk to find out if she was needed, Cassidy quickly headed out of her room and to the lobby of the inn.

The scene she met on her arrival was pure chaos.

Mr. and Mrs. Miller and their twin boys were frantically searching for something. Both boys seemed to be terribly upset, but Logan, the slightly shorter twin, was having a full meltdown.

By now, several other guests were either at the top of the stairs looking down to see what was happening or on their way down the staircase. As Cassidy came into the foyer area, she could also see several guests in both the community room and the dining room, some down on their knees. It was clear something was missing.

Mrs. Miller hustled up to Cassidy, her young face flustered, and rapidly explained that the twins both had a favorite stuffed animal they slept with each night. Logan's was a stuffed rabbit named Baxter, and he was missing. "We know Baxter was on Logan's bunkbed when he got up from his nap. I helped Logan get dressed for our afternoon at the lake. Logan wanted to take Baxter with us but I explained that Baxter didn't like the sand and he'd prefer to stay in the room and play with his best friend, Rex." Seeing that

Cassidy looked confused, Mrs. Miller went on to explain that her other son Mason's favorite stuffed animal was a purple dinosaur called Rex. "Rex was on Mason's bed when the boys got out of their bath and into their pajamas, but Baxter was nowhere to be found."

Cassidy looked up toward the second-floor landing and saw several guests with groggy faces wearing pajamas and robes, all peering downstairs at the scene. A couple of the guests ventured downstairs to get a closer look at what was happening.

To make matters even worse, the twins continued to wail and now their little faces were bright red and both had runny noses and tears streaming down their cheeks. Mrs. Miller was wringing her hands and a few tears streaked her face also.

"I'm so sorry that both the boys are making such a ruckus about this situation," Mrs. Miller continued. "Logan is crying because his stuffed animal is missing, and Mason is crying because Logan accused him of stealing his stuffed animal or throwing it away. It seems the twins had some type of argument over whose idea it was to climb on the rocks the other day, which resulted in us punishing both boys by keeping them inside this afternoon. We needed them to understand they had done something dangerous. For some reason, they decided to argue over it again. Even after the threat of punishment, Mason still says he never touched the rabbit.

"So, after we looked everywhere in our room and the second-floor hallway and still hadn't found Baxter, we decided to search downstairs. We had hoped to find the rabbit by now. We even tried to convince Logan that Baxter must have hidden himself for the night and didn't want to be found until morning to buy us some more time to search for the lost rabbit. We thought that maybe we could get the boys calmed down and into bed. Again, I'm so sorry for the confusion we are causing for your guests. I don't know what else to do at this point."

Mrs. Miller led the twins into the dining room to try and console them by offering any snack they wanted from the large bowl on the counter. She also took a couple of the small cars and trucks out of the toybox and got the boys interested in running them across the rug. This seemed to temporarily calm them down.

Knowing the inn better than her guests, Cassidy joined the search and looked in every place a ten-inch stuffed rabbit could be hidden by an unhappy brother. There were several cabinets in the community room where they stored games and puzzles, so Cassidy headed into the room and got down on her knees to pull out the contents. *Nope, no rabbit.*

Heading back through the dining room Cassidy smiled when she saw Elizabeth and her husband John searching under the table and chairs. She was surprised to see even the senior Connellys downstairs in their robes. Mr. Connelly was looking behind the hutch and Mrs. Connelly was pulling the long drapes covering the windows away from the walls in search of the missing rabbit.

It seemed everyone was involved in the search. It was getting late and Cassidy was starting to worry about the amount of noise and if it was keeping her other guests, a few of whom remained in their rooms upstairs, from sleeping or enjoying a quiet night.

Cassidy returned to the front desk and realized that the twins had stopped crying, at least for now. The search continued, but so far, the missing rabbit hadn't turned up.

Unable to get any work done with all of the ruckus, Jack went to check out what all the commotion was about.

Once he found out he decided to put the sleuthing skills he utilized in some of his books to good use. He figured that by trying to gain the trust of the twins, he could find a few clues to what might have happened to the stuffed animal. Jack could just see his publisher going into spasms of laughter if he ever found out this was how his prized author was spending his "quiet time at the inn"—hunting for lost stuffed animals. But otherwise, no one was going to get any sleep.

Jack joined Mrs. Miller and the twins in the dining room. After a few quick words with the young mom, he got down at eye-level with the boys and reminded both that he had helped them get safely off the rocks and that he was their friend and wanted to help find Baxter. He asked both boys a few questions and he could see that Mason had guilt written all over his face. Jack asked Mason to help him get a drink of water for his brother. As they walked to the dining room Jack said if he were a rabbit, he would probably hide in the refrigerator.

"That is silly. Rabbits don't like to be cold," Mason said perking up to the conversation.

"Wow, you are really smart about what rabbits like. If you were a rabbit, where would you hide?"

Mason paused for a second and then he said, "I might have opened the window by the desk in our room and jumped outside to get some fresh air." Realizing he might have said too much, Mason quickly added, "or I might come back if someone left me some treats. You know, like a carrot. And of course, a cookie. Yep, that is what I think will help Baxter come home. Don't you agree Mr. Burnett?"

Jack tried not to laugh and instead rubbed his finger across his chin and tried to look serious. "I think you may be on to something Mason. For now, why don't you let me handle this and you go back up to your room with your family. I don't think Baxter will come back unless no one is around. You know, kind of like Santa Claus."

After apparently thinking about it for a moment, Mason nodded in agreement and followed Jack back out the foyer to join his parents.

Jack walked over to Cassidy. He couldn't help but stare at her in her bright pink robe and unusual slippers. He knew the second she realized he was staring at her when a red blush rose up her neck. "I'm aware it's really late and a bit unusual but could you put a few cookies on a plate along with a carrot and place them on the small table to the right of the bottom of the staircase?"

"Why would I do that in the middle of this crisis? If you want a snack, there are snacks in the dining room for all the guests. Help yourself," Cassidy said a bit tensely.

Jack studied Cassidy for a minute and then realized he needed to explain further. "I think I can get the twins to head back to bed if I tell them that Baxter is playing Hide-n-Seek with them but that he was so tired he fell asleep in his hiding place. As soon as he gets hungry, he'll come out of hiding to get his snack. He'll see the treats and then go back upstairs to join Logan in bed, but *only* if Logan goes back to bed and is asleep. Baxter doesn't want Logan to know that he can walk on his own. He wants Logan to continue to think he needs to be carried everywhere he goes. Now do you get it?"

It took Cassidy a minute to realize that Jack was serious. "One question, what happens when we can't find the rabbit?"

"From my conversation with the other twin, Mason, I think I know where he hid it. Now that the entire inn is in an uproar, I think Mason is afraid to tell anyone where he hid Baxter. If you play along with me, we might be able to get everyone back to bed and teach Mason a lesson also. Are you okay with my plan?"

"A plate of cookies and a carrot coming right up," Cassidy said over her shoulder as she hurried off to the kitchen to fix the snacks as requested.

Cassidy brought the snacks back and put the plate where Jack instructed her. She saw him lean down to speak to the boys and then they surprisingly each grabbed one of his hands and headed up the stairs, although Logan turned around one last time to look at the snacks sitting on the plate. *Maybe Jack's not such a grumpy guy after all,* she mused.

Everyone else returned to their rooms and the inn was once again quiet. Cassidy remained in the foyer waiting for Jack to return. It seemed like forever until he finally rejoined her. "I was starting to wonder if I was going to have to find Baxter on my own."

"Nope. The boys insisted I tell them a story and I didn't want to risk the peace treaty we achieved, and of course once I saw a quivering lip again on Logan I decided to stay. I didn't get five minutes into a story I made up about a rabbit family who stayed at an inn near a lake when both boys were fast asleep. Mr. and Mrs. Miller were so grateful. I quietly snuck out of the room. Now, let's go find Baxter before those clouds I saw forming earlier turn into rain and it makes it harder to find our man, err, I mean our rabbit," Jack said in a voice slightly higher than a whisper.

He headed towards the front door but stopped and looked down at Cassidy's slippers.

"Do you think you should change your shoes before we go outside?" Jack asked Cassidy, clearly trying to hide a chuckle.

"My puppy dogs have leather bottoms I'll have you know. They are good to go outside."

She noticed Jack glance back up from her slippers into her eyes, but not before his gaze lingered for a second on her pink terrycloth robe. She felt her cheeks flush and she drew it tighter around her. "Just let me grab a jacket to throw over my robe. I keep one in the coat closet to the left of the front door."

Jack led the way out the front door of the inn.

"Where are we headed?" Cassidy questioned.

"Shh," Jack whispered as he grabbed Cassidy's hand so she could follow him along the path to the other side of the inn. Jack kept looking up towards the windows on the second floor and when he got to the last set, he turned towards Cassidy. "The Millers are on the opposite end of the hall from me, so I assume the windows above us are the ones by the boys' bed, right?"

"One more window down, the one on the corner would be the window by the twin's bunkbed."

Jack dropped Cassidy's hand and told her to stay still. He walked over to the bushes along the front wall and squeezed himself into the space between the brush and the foundation of the building. He came out again onto the walkway a couple of bushes down.

"I didn't find anything," Jack whispered. "I think I need to squeeze behind the next section of bushes." Jack again vanished out of sight, but Cassidy could hear him moving along the wall and she could see the plants moving slightly as Jack pushed deeper along the hedge.

"Jack, are you okay?" Cassidy whispered. Receiving no response, she asked again, "Jack?" *That's all I need is to lose a guest*, she worried.

About that time Cassidy saw Jack emerge from the bushes with something in his hand, but the clouds blocked out the light from the moon, so it was hard to see. When he finally joined her on the walkway she could clearly see it was a stuffed rabbit—a bit dirty but it seemed to be in one piece.

Cassidy had never been happier to see a dirty toy in her life as she was in that moment. Without thinking she reached over and hugged Jack, throwing her arms tightly around his neck. She felt his arms circle around her waist in return and it felt so good and so right that she lingered there for a minute before moving back a few inches and looking up into his eyes.

It wasn't clear who was more surprised, Cassidy or Jack.

Cassidy stood still, frozen, unable to move away. She realized she desperately wanted Jack to kiss her.

Jack also seemed frozen as he gazed into her eyes and for a moment, he seemed to lean toward her, his lips moving closer…and then he abruptly dropped his hands and backed up a few feet.

Cassidy's first reaction was disappointment but then she

realized that they had both been caught up in the moment. She just as quickly realized he could have finished the kiss and then apologized. She wasn't *that* unappealing. She'd been told her lips looked very "kissable" in the past by several of her boyfriends. She assumed Mr. Burnett must not feel the same way.

Jack took a few steps back but didn't say anything so now Cassidy was totally embarrassed. She felt like she had made a fool of herself. Cassidy couldn't get back down the walkway fast enough and her overstuffed slippers were not helping her speed. She needed time to think, and she needed to splash some cold water on her face to remove the red flush she still felt on her cheeks.

Once inside the inn Cassidy went off to take the rabbit to the kitchen to clean him up, leaving Jack standing in the foyer watching her walk down the hallway in those ridiculously adorable slippers. *What had just happened?* He had recently sworn off all women. He'd been burned one too many times. He needed to keep a clear head and finish his book.

What was I thinking? The problem was, he *hadn't* been thinking in that moment. He'd let his emotions take over and then belatedly realized that this could only spell trouble for him.

Jack walked over to the plate of snacks left out for Baxter and he absently started eating the treats. He picked up the tray and walked over to sit on the bottom step of the stairway to the second floor. When he reached down for another chocolate chip cookie, he was shocked to see that he had eaten everything on the tray, including the carrot.

Jack got up and walked back over to the front desk, placing the empty tray on the corner. His mind was spinning. What should he do now? Should he speak to Cassidy about what almost happened outside? Should he just pretend it didn't happen? Yes, he'd just play it cool when Cassidy returned. He'd pretend nothing had happened. Yes, that was the right strategy overall—pretend like nothing happened.

When Cassidy reached the kitchen, she turned on the light and moved over to the sink. Grabbing a wet kitchen cloth, she began to wipe away the dirt from the stuffed rabbit. Realizing the toy was damp, she walked down the hall to her personal suite and grabbed her hair dryer. The hum of the dryer and the mindless motion of her hand waving it back and forth allowed Cassidy's mind to wander. *Why did I hug Jack? Why did he hug me back? Was he just as surprised and it was an automatic reaction? Did I want him to kiss me?*

Yes, she realized, she very much wanted Jack to kiss her, and she was hurt when he pushed her away. Maybe her first impression of him was right. He was a grumpy recluse and she needed to stay clear of him going forward or she would get her heart broken. Darn, how had her heart gotten engaged so quickly? She hadn't even realized she was falling for him.

Cassidy was hoping when she went back to the foyer to return the rabbit that Jack would explain his behavior or even say that he was just caught off guard. Yes, that was it. Jack just needed time to realize that there was a spark between them during the embrace on the walkway. Once he'd had time to calm down, he would be ready to make the next move. Maybe even ask Cassidy out on a real date. Maybe finish the kiss they were meant to have outside.

Jack was standing at the front desk when Cassidy returned with the refreshed Baxter. She put a big smile on her face and was glad that she'd taken a few extra minutes to brush her hair and wash her face.

"Here is the runaway rabbit, all clean and smelling a lot better. How do you plan to get him back in the room? Do you need me to go up with you and use my room key to open the door slightly so you can sneak the rabbit inside the room?" *Anything to stay with Jack for a few more minutes,* she thought, hoping a kiss was coming.

"That won't be necessary," Jack said bluntly. "I arranged with the Millers to lightly tap on their door so Mr. Miller could take the rabbit and put it in bed with Logan. Or if I didn't find the rabbit, I'd send him a text before I went back to my room for the night. I'll take care of this and then I plan to head straight to my room. My work is waiting for me."

The abrupt change in Jack's emotions stunned Cassidy. Feelings of hurt and disappointment welled up in her. She almost jumped when Jack's hand slightly brushed hers as he was reaching for the stuffed animal. Again, she was disappointed when Jack quickly pulled his hand back after securing Baxter. He turned and started to go upstairs. Cassidy couldn't believe he wasn't going to say anything about what happened outside.

Jack stopped on the second step and turned around to look at her. "Thank you for your help Cassidy. I wouldn't have known how to clean the rabbit as well as you did. I'm sure the Millers will thank you in the morning. I wanted to…" Jack suddenly stopped in mid-sentence. He hesitated for a brief second and she could see a flurry of emotions running across his face, but when he spoke, he seemed to have changed his mind and instead said, "Goodnight Cassidy and thanks again for your help. I'll be working around the clock the next few days, so I won't be down for breakfast. Oh, and I also won't need my room cleaned for a couple of days, thanks." Jack almost ran up the remainder of the steps.

Cassidy heard the light knock on the Millers door and a hushed conversation. She remained standing still at the bottom of the stairs until she heard the door to Room #5 open and shut. She looked up the stairs and waited to see if Jack was coming back down. After staring at an empty set of stairs for several moments, she realized he wasn't. She had read his emotions outside on the walkway incorrectly and had made a fool of herself.

Walking back to her suite, Cassidy replayed the scene over and over again in her head. She was sure she'd seen the same desire in Jack's eyes as she had felt. *How could I have been so wrong?* she asked herself. But wrong she was. She realized the best thing she could do now was just stuff down her feelings and get some sleep.

Slipping into her bed, Cassidy pulled the covers up to her chin and thought about her journey to get this far. Grams always popped into her mind in moments like these. She missed her grandmother's smiling face and her big warm hugs. Grams always had solid advice to share. Cassidy sure could use a hug and some advice right now.

Cassidy looked up towards the window and could see a flash of lightening peep through the closed curtains. Was it a coincidence or was that Grams sending her a message?

Either way, it reminded her again of the last words Grams ever said to her, which made her smile. Cassidy looked up and said "*Hi Grams, I get it—you are reminding me it's time to get some sleep. Tomorrow is another day to live my life, do good in the world and make you proud. And yes, I'll remember to smile.* And, with that, Cassidy dozed off into a deep sleep.

CHAPTER 9

When Jack got back to his room, his head was full of competing thoughts.

He thought about the scene outside and his unexpected emotions. He thought about the hurt look on Cassidy's face when he pulled away from her embrace and then again when he left her standing in the foyer to return to his room. He remembered the abrupt little speech he made about not coming down for breakfast. He felt guilty, but at the same time, he'd done the right thing. He needed space and wasn't ready to get entangled with Cassidy or any woman for that matter. He needed to remain totally focused on finishing his book.

On the other hand, the missing stuffed animal and the chaotic scene he found when he walked downstairs earlier in the evening also started swirling around in his head. Something clicked. His brain finally engaged, and he was surprised to find that a potential storyline was forming for his final chapters. The more he thought it through, the better it seemed.

Jack quickly pulled out his laptop and reread the start of the chapter where he had gotten stuck and couldn't find a way to move forward. He was looking for a way for his villain to sneak contraband out of the country. Maybe it would work. Jack started hitting the keys and within an hour he had a rough outline of the last third of the book. The more he built on the outline, the better he liked the flow. Jack even decided to name the latest character Special Agent Baxter. No one would believe how this latest storyline was born and he didn't plan on sharing that little tidbit with anyone.

Realizing it was going to be a long night, Jack walked over to the kitchenette in his room and made himself a strong cup of black coffee. As he waited for it to brew, his mind kept jumping back to Cassidy. He knew he had to shut down those images and emotions. But he couldn't seem to do it. Her big, beautiful brown eyes and the sweet sound of her laughter kept barging into his thoughts. He couldn't seem to get her out of his mind. Jack didn't think that Cassidy realized how beautiful she really was. It wasn't only her looks but the way she genuinely cared about her inn, her guests, and the town. That woman had a lot of passion for life and Jack started to wonder what it would be like if she shared that passion with him.

Jack knew he needed to stop acting like a smitten teenager. Before he allowed himself to continue with this line of thinking, he had a book to finish. Book first, romance next. Get the book done and then go after Cassidy to see if there was any possibility of a relationship between the two of them.

Taking his coffee back to the desk Jack sat down and amazingly, the entire story started to unfold on his screen. He planned to finish a chapter and then get some sleep, but once he finished that chapter, the words kept flowing so Jack kept at it. He looked at his watch: it was past midnight. He'd stop in another few minutes, for sure.

Ding. Ding. Ding. The clock in the community room chimed out three more times. A few more hours passed. The only person awake in the entire inn was the guest in Room #5.

Just two hours later Cassidy's alarm went off. The start to another day. Typically, she jumped right out of bed, but today she continued to lay there for a while. She kept thinking about how close she had come to making a total fool of herself the previous night. Today she planned to stay away from Jack and find creative ways to avoid him whenever possible.

Quickly going through her morning routine Cassidy stayed focused on the long list of things to do. Most of the items were routine and easy to accomplish. The items related to operating an inn were often time-consuming, but they were things she could do on autopilot. The items related to the Lakeview Hospital Annual Gala required a bit more thought and careful planning. Cassidy decided to break out the gala related items to a separate list so she could drill down a bit deeper.

The first item to tackle today, however, was to get through another breakfast without Peter. One more day and he would be back at work at the inn and her life would go back to "normal" which to most people would still be called hectic—but at least it was routine.

Once breakfast was done and the hired crew was hard at work on cleaning the rooms, Cassidy went into her office to tackle the ever-growing stack of paperwork, ordering, and checking the inn's website for feedback from prior guests.

The next couple of hours flew by and Cassidy was happy with her progress. She didn't want Peter to come back to an empty pantry or limited supplies, so she had taken care of the ordering first. With that done, she moved on to checking the bookings, which were in line with what she expected. The last item was checking the former guests' reviews on the website.

First, Cassidy needed another strong cup of coffee so she helped herself to the last bit in the kitchen's large industrial size pot and then took the time to give it a good cleaning and shined the outside. Peter wouldn't have anything to complain about, hopefully.

Going back to her desk Cassidy finally pulled up the reviews. She was so happy to see their high ratings, but one comment caught her eye. The guest had just checked out that morning, so she was surprised to see the rating was already posted. An immediate review typically meant that the guest either had a great visit or he or she was unhappy or had experienced something that didn't meet expectations.

Cassidy quickly opened the online review and read it through: 'We had a wonderful stay at the Crystal Lake Inn over the past week. With five-year-old twin boys, we weren't sure that staying at a quaint inn would work. Our boys have so much energy and they always seem to find ways to get into trouble. Yet, at the inn, everyone was so nice, and no one seemed to be bothered by two little boys. Our hostess, Cassidy, and another guest, Jack, went out of their way to help us find a missing stuffed rabbit that our son can't sleep without. Jack came to our rescue and found the missing toy and Cassidy washed away the dirt and the toy was as good as new. On an earlier day in our stay, Jack also went out of his way to keep our boys safe when they ventured out of our immediate view. We can't thank them enough for treating us like family. We've already booked again next year. We are giving the inn and our experience five stars. Mr. and Mrs. Miller'.

A big smile formed on Cassidy's face. The Millers were kind to not only give a five-star rating, but to also write such a touching note. The review made Cassidy's day a bit brighter, although it didn't do anything to help her heart, especially the mention of Jack and how kind he had been, not just once, but twice. Jack's kindness touched her heart too—but he'd made it quite clear that he was not interested in Cassidy in a romantic way. Oh well, she told herself, I'm too busy to add something else to my plate right now anyway…even if that something else had beautiful baby blue eyes. Cassidy took a deep breath and did a slow exhale. She repeated this a couple of times to clear her head and get her heart rate back to a normal level. Then, she turned back to her desk to tackle the ever-present pile of paperwork that was calling her name.

Sometime around five a.m., Jack finally fell asleep. He was happy with the progress he'd made with his writing and he literally passed out. He didn't even remember his head hitting the pillow before he was asleep, so he shouldn't have been surprised when he woke up to a strong ray of sunlight peeking through his drawn curtains. When he put his feet over the side of the bed to put on his slippers, he noticed they were not where he typically left them. Still sitting on the bed, he did a visual look around his room, yet he didn't see them anywhere. He then noticed two rectangular bumps under the blankets. He pulled back the blankets and saw that his slippers were in the bed. Apparently, he'd been so tired the night before that he forgot to remove his slippers and they ended up in bed with him. He must have kicked them off in the night.

Retrieving his slippers Jack made sure his DO NOT DISTURB sign was on the outside of his door and then headed to the bathroom for a much-needed shower. Next, he fixed a strong cup of coffee and grabbed a yogurt from the mini fridge in his room and sat down at the desk.

As soon as Jack sat down, Cassidy crossed his mind. Recalling the scene from the previous night made his heart beat faster. As hard as Jack tried to wipe Cassidy from his mind, he just couldn't seem to do it. Maybe he would go downstairs and ask her if they could grab a cup of coffee or take a walk.

Jack was still trying to decide if he wanted to seek her out when he heard Cassidy's voice in the hallway. He could hear her talking with one of the guests who was asking for directions to her friend Trish's gift shop in town.

He quickly decided to take advantage of Cassidy being right outside his door. He was going to ask her if they could meet in town for coffee that afternoon. Before he lost his nerve, Jack opened the door to his room and stepped into the hallway.

As soon as Cassidy saw him, she looked away to finish giving directions. Jack detected a nervous look on her face. Or was she annoyed? Satisfied, the guest walked away, and the innkeeper grabbed several towels off the linen cart and headed toward him. "Mr. Burnett, did you need something? Maybe some fresh towels?"

"I, umm, ah…" Jack couldn't get his mouth to work properly. Finally, he came to his senses. "I know things got a little complicated last night and I feel badly about the way the evening ended. I was wondering if you would like to join me at The Perk in about an hour for a cup of coffee?" Jack held his breath while waiting for her response.

Cassidy appeared to be stunned, hesitating for a moment. Jack's heart thudded in his chest until she finally spoke.

"Yes, I'd like to join you for a cup of coffee. I can be ready to go in an hour. First, I have a few things to wrap up here. How about I meet you at The Perk at, let's say, one o'clock. Will that work for you?"

"Perfect. That will give me time to walk down Main Street and check out a few of the stores." Jack gave Cassidy a big smile and waved goodbye as he turned around and walked back into his room. He realized he was excited that Cassidy said yes. With an hour to kill, he opened his laptop hoping to get a bit more work done before he walked into town. Jack didn't get more than two additional paragraphs written when his cellphone rang. Seeing it was his publisher, Thornton Reed, he frowned, but answered the call.

"Good morning Thornton. Why are you calling me so early in the morning?"

"Jack, it's twelve-thirty and that classifies as the afternoon. Did you just get up?"

Jack blew out an exaggerated breath so Thornton would know he was already tired of the conversation. "Get to the point. What can I do for you?"

"How's the last part of your book coming? You know I don't like to hound you, but the pressure is on. Have you made any progress?"

"You might be surprised to hear that I had a breakthrough. I was up until five this morning updating my outline and filling in the storyline. I've made some significant progress and came up with a brilliant way for my villain to sneak the contraband out of the country. I think you'll like the direction the story is headed. So now that you know I'm back on track, is there anything else I can do for you today?"

"I wanted to go over the details of the charity event I mentioned to you a few weeks ago. The plans are finalized, and a car service will be picking you up. Grab a pen so you can write down the name and address of where you'll be staying." After a pause, Thornton asked, "Jack, can you hold on for a minute, my assistant just walked into the room."

Jack could hear muffled talk between Thornton and his assistant. He looked at his watch and realized that he needed to be at The Perk in ten minutes.

"Thornton," Jack called into his cell. "Did you forget I'm on the line?"

"Sorry Jack. I've got to run. It seems the legal department has some issue that needs my immediate attention. I'll call you back later. Got to run. Goodbye."

Jack realized he was now listening to dead air, so he pushed the red disconnect button. Happy to get off the line, Jack decided to change his shirt before going downstairs. As he reached for his cell phone to put it in his pocket, it rang and he saw it was Thornton again.

"You again? I'm beginning to think that you don't have any other clients except me. What's up?"

"Jack, you are not going to like this, but your lawyer and our corporate lawyers have been in a heated battle for the past two days on a few clauses in your contract. It's not pretty. I wouldn't ask this if I didn't think it was necessary, but I need you to come back to the city immediately. Trouble is brewing and it's in your best interest to be at the table to help clear up a fairly big issue with your royalty clauses."

"Are you kidding me? How can that be? We're on book number three of that deal. I trust you to do the right thing by me. I can't be running back to the city and also keep my writing flowing. Do you really think it's that important that I come back immediately?"

"Yes. Yes, I do, or I wouldn't have called you to ask you to come back. I can only stall them until first thing in the morning at the latest, but I'd prefer to pull a meeting together for early this evening if possible. I don't even know where you are. Can you get back in four or five hours?"

Jack could tell by the tone of Thornton's voice that the situation was serious. After pausing for a couple of seconds to think through his options, Jack decided that it was in his best interest to be in person at the meeting versus a video call. He'd just have to jump in his car and head to the city.

"I can be in your office by six tonight. Get the meeting arranged. You can call me while I'm on the road to give me more details about the issue so I'm better prepared. I'll also need to call my lawyer while I'm on the way."

Thornton thanked Jack for agreeing to come to his office that evening and hung up. Jack quickly started to put his laptop and several other items he would need for his trip into his briefcase and his small overnight bag. He wouldn't take the time to pack since he could go to his condo in New York that night to sleep and shower. He planned to be back in Lakeview by the following afternoon.

Jack dialed the front desk so he could tell Cassidy about the change in plans, but when someone answered, it was her friend Trish.

"Hi Trish. This is Jack Burnett in Room #5. I'd like to speak to Cassidy, please."

"I'm sorry but she just left. She was heading into town to meet someone at The Perk. Can I take a message?" Trish offered.

"Do you have a way to reach her? Please let her know that I won't be able to meet her for coffee. Something came up and I need to return to the city for a day. Maybe two at the most. I'd like to stay checked into my room, if possible."

Trish needed a moment to process this news. She knew Cassidy was going into town to meet someone for coffee, but it seemed her friend left out this juicy tidbit of information. "Yes, Mr. Burnett, we can keep your room for you, and I'll be sure to give Cassidy your message."

Jack thought about how impersonal it was to ask Cassidy's friend to relay his message. "Trish, on second thought, I'd prefer to write Cassidy a personal note and give her details. Will you just tell her that I couldn't make it to the coffee shop and let her know that I'm leaving a note in my room for her. Is that okay?"

"Yes, that works. Just leave the note on the desk in your room. I'll let her know to look for it when she gets back to the inn."

"Thanks so much." Jack hung up and hurried downstairs and into his car. The quicker he got on the road and on his way to the city, the quicker he could be back to sort things out with Cassidy.

CHAPTER 10

Trish tried Cassidy's cellphone several times, but each time the call went to voicemail, so she left a brief message. "Hi Cassidy, this is Trish. Mr. Burnett said something came up and he wouldn't be able to meet you for coffee. Also, I need to leave immediately. I left the part-time clerk at the front desk. What started out as a minor plumbing leak at my gift store has now turned into a bigger issue and the plumber is on the way to the shop. I've got to run. I'll talk to you later...."

Not wanting to be late, Cassidy arrived at The Perk a few minutes early and ordered her usual, an Americano. She could smell the rich aroma as soon as she lifted the lid to add her extra shot of cream. Taking a long sip of the hot liquid, Cassidy looked around to see if Jack was already seated. Not seeing him in the café, she spotted an empty seat near the window. From that vantage point she could see Jack as soon as he arrived.

Cassidy decided to turn her cell phone on mute so she wouldn't be interrupted during her coffee with Jack. For the next two hours Trish would easily handle whatever came up at the inn. She turned the phone face down on the table so she wouldn't be tempted to constantly look at it.

Several of Cassidy's friends and other members of the Lakeview Business Association stopped by to chat with her.

Cassidy looked at her watch and noticed that Jack was now fifteen minutes late. She was getting a little concerned. Did she misunderstand? She replayed the conversation in her head and was sure she had the time correct. Maybe he got tied up on a call. A few other locals stopped by to chat and before she even realized it Jack was now forty minutes late.

Main Street was only three blocks long so Cassidy didn't think Jack could still be window shopping. She walked over to the front door, stepped outside and looked up and down the street. She didn't see Jack anywhere.

Walking back into the coffee shop, Cassidy saw the entire Connelly family walking towards her. She stopped so that she could say hello.

"Hello, Connelly family. It looks like you're enjoying our fine weather. I hope you're also enjoying your last day in Lakeview." Cassidy genuinely liked this family, and she was happy they'd decided to stay again this year, even with the baby on the way.

"Yes, Cassidy," Mr. Connelly said with a bright smile. "We've been doing a little shopping as you can see from all these bags. It seems, somehow, that I got stuck carrying most of them. I only bought one thing, but I have six bags to carry."

"You know you love to be the one waiting on a bench while we browse the shops," Mrs. Connelly chimed in. "We love all the little specialty shops in town. We especially loved Gifts on Main. Your friend Trish was so helpful. We even got this adorable little onesie for our grandchild. Mrs. Connelly pulled a cute one-piece undershirt from a bag. It had, 'Grandpop is my favorite' printed on it. "Now, who do you think bought this?"

Mr. Connelly cleared his throat and quickly changed the subject by saying, "we are headed to the bistro for a light lunch. Then it's time for us to get Elizabeth back to the inn for her afternoon nap."

"And our afternoon nap," Mrs. Connelly added. "We'll see you for the "Sit-n-Sip' this evening."

Cassidy waved as the family walked away. Taking one more look for Jack and not seeing him, she walked back into The Perk and sat down for a few more minutes.

Cassidy went from being a bit concerned to being frustrated. If Jack couldn't make it, he at least could have called her. Cassidy's phone number was plastered all over the front desk and the website.

Turning her phone over she saw a voicemail from Trish and assumed it was something related to the inn. But there was nothing from Jack, so she didn't listen to the voicemail. Now she was moving from feeling frustrated and hurt to being angry.

By the time Jack was officially over an hour late, Cassidy was fuming. She threw away her now empty coffee cup and marched out of The Perk and got into her car, where she sat for a few minutes. She decided to listen to her voicemail from Trish, making sure that everything was okay at the inn. Being the somewhat clumsy person she was known to be, while trying to play the voicemail, Cassidy accidentally hit the delete button.

"Oh darn," Cassidy said out loud. She tried to un-delete the voicemail, but only ended up permanently deleting it. Now her frustration was beyond words so she decided to go back to the inn to see if she could find Jack and see why he stood her up.

Arriving back at the inn, Cassidy found a note on the front desk from Trish with a few requests from their current guests and another saying there was a plumbing problem at her shop in town, but no note that mentioned Jack.

Cassidy went to find him. She knocked on his door several times without any response. As she turned to leave, another guest saw Cassidy standing at the door to Room #5 and asked if she was looking for the guest in that room. They didn't know the man's name, but they saw him leave about ninety minutes ago with a small bag and his briefcase. It looked like he was in a hurry.

Thanking the guest for the news about Jack, she debated about going into his room and trying to determine if he took all his belongings with him or not. Deciding that wouldn't be right since he had the DO NOT DISTURB sign hanging on the doorknob, Cassidy went back downstairs to deal with the things Trish had left notes about. Once she completed dealing with the special requests she went back to her office.

Cassidy tried to call Trish but got her voicemail. She then called Trish's gift shop, Gifts on Main. She asked to speak to Trish but one of the employees said there was a plumbing problem and Trish and one of the other shop employees were in the restrooms cleaning up the water from a broken pipe. She left a message for Trish to call her, but it seemed like her friend had her hands full, so Cassidy didn't expect to hear back from her any time soon.

Trying to concentrate on her work was useless. Cassidy closed her laptop and walked into the kitchen to start making her treats for the daily Sit-n-Sip held on the front porch. She decided to add something special to the menu and made one of her favorites, warm artichoke dip and toasted crostini slices. She also made her chocolate chip cookies and got the drink cart in order. Once she had everything ready for later that afternoon, she went back to her office.

Cassidy tried to get back to the never-ending pile of paperwork, but her mind kept wandering to Jack. She was sure there was a spark between them and yet this was the second time in two days that Cassidy was disappointed that Jack didn't seem to feel the same way she did. She knew better than to get involved with a guest. She also knew to stick with her instincts. Jack might have shown a softer side with the Miller twins, but now she realized it was fleeting at best. His rude behavior the day he arrived now also included being inconsiderate of her time and her emotions.

Cassidy didn't have time to waste on playing games or catering to giant egos. Whatever Jack was hiding he could just keep it to himself. She was no longer interested. Yep.

Cassidy was done with Jack. Done. Done. *Done.*

The next morning was a beautiful one. The predawn darkness erupted into ribbons of light purple and pink and the temperature was already climbing into the promise of an absolutely gorgeous late spring day. Cassidy loved this time of day and often stole a few minutes of quiet time sitting on the front porch, drinking her first coffee.

Most of her guests wouldn't be downstairs for at least another hour or two. She had time to relax and enjoy the beauty of the scenery around the inn and the view across the lawn to the lake. As the sun finally made its appearance, the reflection on the lake was stunning. Mornings like these quickly reminded Cassidy why she loved her inn, the town and the lake.

Cassidy went back inside to get the breakfast buffet started. She missed Peter and their morning routine. Providing a great start to her guests' day was always a pleasant way to show how much she cared about them. Without Peter, her mornings were a lot more hectic, and she didn't get to spend as much time with her guests as normal. Today would be a little quieter as several guests had checked out yesterday and more would leave after having breakfast this morning, including the Connelly family.

As Cassidy walked into the dining room to fill the heated servicing dishes, she saw that Mr. and Mrs. Connelly were already at the table, but John and Elizabeth were not yet downstairs. Pleasantries were exchanged and Cassidy took the time to refill coffee cups. As she filled Mrs. Connelly's cup, Cassidy noticed that Mrs. Connelly seemed distracted.

"I hope you've had a good stay. It was great having you with us again this year and I enjoyed getting to know Elizabeth," Cassidy said as she moved over to refill Mr. Connelly's cup. "I missed saying goodbye to your daughter Isa and her husband Bruce yesterday when they checked out. I heard they were headed down to Portland for a few days. I hope they enjoyed their stay with us too."

Cassidy noticed that worried looks were exchanged between the two elderly guests. She wondered if something was wrong and debated whether she should pry or not. Wondering if there might be a problem related to Isa and Bruce's stay, Cassidy decided to ask if she could help with anything before they checked out.

Mr. Connelly was quick to speak up. "We all enjoyed our stay. It was good for everyone to get away for a few days. You always make us feel welcome. It reminds me of going to the lake house my family had when I was young, when my grandparents were still with us. All of our aunts, uncles and cousins spent two weeks together. I have such wonderful memories of those vacations. It's one of the reasons I'm so delighted that our children and their spouses join us here.

"And so you know, we'll be booking with you again for next year. I was hoping we could book that larger family suite you mentioned. By the time we come back, we'll have our newest addition and with the adjoining room we could help take care of the baby while our son and his wife get a bit of time to themselves." However, Cassidy still noticed that Mrs. Connelly seemed concerned.

"Of course, I'm fairly sure that we have a few weeks next year around this same time where all of those rooms are available. Why don't I go check now while it's rather quiet in here?" Cassidy went to the front desk to use the computer. Looking at the online reservations for the same time next year Cassidy saw that those rooms were indeed available. She was happy she could give the Connellys the good news and could confirm the dates with them. When she turned around to return to the dining room, Cassidy noticed that Mrs. Connelly was standing at the front desk, still looking worried, which wasn't like her.

"Mrs. Connelly is there something I can help you with this morning? I don't mean to overstep, but you seem to be worried about something."

"My husband always tells me I worry too much, and I guess he's right. It's only...well, I heard Elizabeth and John talking in the night several times. We agreed last night to leave right after breakfast, but they haven't come down yet. I wanted to stop by their room before we came downstairs but it seemed quiet in there and my husband said I should leave them alone. Maybe they were still asleep after their late night. I can feel it though...something isn't right. John would normally text me if they were running late. Now I'm worried."

Cassidy could tell that Mrs. Connelly was getting more concerned as the minutes clicked by on the old grandfather clock in the hallway. Maybe Mrs. Connelly was just a nervous grandmother, or perhaps there was something going on upstairs.

Thinking about her options, Cassidy decided she wanted to ease Mrs. Connelly's fears and she offered to call John's room to see if they wanted her to come help them bring down their luggage. Mrs. Connelly nodded in approval.

"Hi John, it's Cassidy," she said pleasantly into the hotel phone. "Your parents have finished their breakfast and I know you're all getting ready to leave soon, so I'm just calling to let you know I'd be happy to come up and bring down your bags while you and Elizabeth go into the dining room to enjoy your last breakfast with us this trip."

There was a hesitation on the phone and Cassidy immediately knew something wasn't right by the tone of John's voice. Her stomach dropped at the words John spoke. "Elizabeth had a difficult night. She was uncomfortable and not able to sleep. This morning around five she finally dozed off, only to wake back up about an hour ago with significant lower back pain. We put a call into her doctor who just called us back. Our doctor thinks

Elizabeth is in the early stages of labor. I don't think we'll be leaving today."

Before Cassidy could say anything, John asked, "Do you see my parents? I was in the process of calling them when your call came through. Can you ask them to come upstairs? Don't scare them. Just tell them we need some help with luggage or something. I don't want to upset them. This is one of the situations they were worried about, but we researched the local hospital just in case and our doctor has a colleague here in Lakeview, so he was comfortable with this trip."

"John, your mother is standing right next to me, and your father just walked out of the dining room," Cassidy said in a calm voice, glancing up at Mrs. Connelly and smiling." Of course, I'll ask them to come up and help you get ready to leave. No problem. You have my cell number if you need anything. Don't hesitate to call me."

Cassidy didn't even get the chance to say anything to Mrs. Connelly. One look at Cassidy's face and the older woman, a retired nurse, knew exactly what was going on. Without a word she moved swiftly up the stairs, not even waiting for the elevator. As she was running, she called for her husband to follow her. She also asked Cassidy to follow them in case they needed assistance.

Cassidy's heart rate sped up so fast that she could feel the blood pulsing in her head. She followed the Connellys up the stairs and noticed that Mrs. Connelly didn't go immediately into her son's room, which she thought was odd. First, she went into her own room and came out with a small leather bag. Cassidy wasn't sure what was in it, but she assumed it was important. She waited outside the guest room door. It seemed like it took forever, but finally Mrs. Connelly came out and confirmed that Elizabeth was in the early stages of labor, but they had plenty of time.

Cassidy asked what she could do and offered to call the paramedics.

Mrs. Connelly smiled but shook her head no. "No dear, we don't need the paramedics. We have time and I'm glad we're only ten minutes from the regional hospital. I don't think I mentioned this, but I was a labor and delivery nurse for twenty years before I retired. I've seen nervous fathers and grandfathers before, but it's my first time at being a grandmother. My professional instincts have taken over and will help us until we get to the hospital. I still carry some of my medical tools in a small bag, so I was able to check Elizabeth's vitals and she's doing fine. I'm more worried about my husband and John. They both seem to be in a tizzy."

It was clear that Mrs. Connelly was a take-charge kind of person. She called out orders to everyone, including Cassidy, whom she asked to take Mr. Connelly downstairs with her to get him out of the way. She also asked Cassidy to pack them several bottles of water and a few snacks and then asked her husband to move the car up to the front door.

As Cassidy and Mr. Connelly were halfway down the stairs, Cassidy could hear Mrs. Connelly speaking softly to Elizabeth telling her everything was going to be fine, that they had plenty of time to get to the local hospital which was close by, and that her vitals were good. "Elizabeth, we probably have several hours before the baby arrives," she heard her continue. "The most important thing for you to do is to try to stay calm. Once we get you to the hospital, we'll see if you can get a bit of rest. You're going to need it later. Don't worry about the rest of us. I'll be there to keep everyone else calm."

How Mrs. Connelly stayed so calm was beyond Cassidy. She never had a baby born at the inn and she was glad today wouldn't be the first time. She did as Mrs. Connelly told her and was waiting by the car when Elizabeth came outside.

"We had a delightful stay," Elizabeth said as she gave Cassidy a big hug. "I wanted to thank you for taking such good care of us. I hope you can hold our rooms for a few more days, but right now it looks like I have something rather urgent to take care—I need to give my husband a son and our parents their first grandson."

"A grandson! Did you hear that everyone? We're having a grandson!" Mr. Connelly yelled to anyone who was within shouting distance.

As calm as Mrs. Connelly had been up to this point, Cassidy could now see a few tears trickling down her face. It seemed this bit of news over-rode her nurse's professionalism and invoked the emotions of a grandmother. But then she quickly reverted to nurse mode again and switched into high gear, telling her husband to hurry and get in the car.

The grandparents were already in the backseat when John turned to Elizabeth and in a very calm but direct way said, "Darling, I really think we need to go now. Please get in the car or someone will be picking me up off the driveway." John gently guided his wife into the car.

"Don't worry, your rooms will be here for as long as you need them. Please let me know if there is anything I can do for any of you. And don't forget to call us when the newest Connelly arrives." Even as Cassidy was finishing her sentence, the car drove down the driveway.

Cassidy stood there for a few minutes and breathed deeply, trying to slow down her rapidly beating heart. As she turned to look back at the inn, she saw several other guests standing out on the porch. She needed to go speak with them and let them know everything was fine.

"It's good news, the Connellys are on their way to the hospital to bring their baby son into this world. Fortunately, the grandmother was a labor and delivery nurse, so she had everything under control." There was a round of applause and smiles from those assembled on the porch. "Let's go inside and have breakfast, everyone."

As Cassidy went back into the kitchen to refill some of the buffet items she thought about the crazy morning and was glad that everything seemed to be getting back to normal. Of course, this was something else that Peter missed. He always said that nothing exciting happened at Crystal Lake Inn and Cassidy always reminded him that was a good thing.

Peter missed the excitement of the morning and Cassidy missed him. She knew he'd be back soon, and no one would be happier than she would be to turn the kitchen back over to her head chef.

A few hours later Cassidy got a text message on her phone that said John Connelly Junior had arrived. Mother and son were fine. A second later a picture of a small red-faced baby, tightly swaddled in a blue baby blanket, also arrived. It was times like these that Cassidy wondered if her day at motherhood would ever come. That thought always brought a moment of sadness to her heart. She could hear her grandmother's words in her head: "Your day will come my dear. Your heart will tell you when you've found Mr. Right and I'm sure that my great grandbabies will be along soon afterwards."

CHAPTER 11

The morning flew by. Cassidy had grabbed another cup of coffee and was on the phone with Sarah Jenkins, reordering a case of hand-painted coffee mugs. "I can't believe how fast your items are selling. At this rate, we may need to think about an automatic reorder, at least for the high traffic months."

"That's a great idea. I have a few other clients on automatic reordering. It reduces the time we spend on administrative tasks, and we can spend more time being creative—which we all love." Sarah asked Cassidy a few more questions and confirmed the special merchandise for the VIP weekend would be delivered on time.

Before she had time to catch her breath, the grandfather clock was chiming twelve o'clock noon and Cassidy was busy checking out guests, settling accounts and helping people with directions and other small requests.

Later than she intended, she got back into the kitchen after checking on the cleaning crew upstairs. Cassidy wanted to put extra effort into getting the kitchen ready to turn back over to Peter. He was due back in a few hours so Cassidy wanted everything to be spotless. Wiping down Peter's work counter one more time, she stepped back and took a good look around. Everything was well stocked, and the counters and appliances were shining.

"It's good to see you finally doing some work around here," Peter said jokingly as he strolled into the kitchen, rolling his suitcase behind him. His wavy blonde hair was longer than normal and today it looked wind-blown and messy. "I should have stayed away longer. Everything seems like it's in perfect order. Maybe you don't really need me here after all."

"OMG. No one is happier to see you back than me, except for a few of our repeat guests who missed your delicious meals. Regrettably, some of our current guests don't know what they're missing. Now that you're back, they will be wowed for sure."

Cassidy walked over and gave Peter a big hug. They'd been friends for six years. She had first met Peter when he was head chef at a small boutique hotel in the Adirondacks. Grams had taken Cassidy on a weeklong trip that included a four day stay at a very posh spa, which also had a fantastic restaurant. Peter was the new chef, and his food was outrageously good. So good in fact that they ate almost every meal at the hotel.

When Grams offered to treat Cassidy and her two best friends to a girls' weekend at that same inn and spa as a college graduation gift, they gladly accepted. It was on the second visit to the inn that Cassidy accidently ran into Peter while jogging on one of the local trails; literally, ran into him. Fortunately, neither of them was hurt but they decided to meet for coffee later that afternoon.

They talked for hours about their lives, past romances and their dreams for the future. Cassidy was saddened when Peter shared that his first love, Emma, had been killed in a terrible automobile accident that also took the lives of her parents. He had struggled to move forward with his life for months. But then the job at the upscale spa and restaurant was offered to him and he gladly accepted the position.

At first the new job took his mind off of Emma and what he had lost, but then, he shared that he was disillusioned by the strict structure of the management at the inn. He was looking for a smaller inn where he could cook simple, yet high quality meals and still enjoy his second passion of outdoor sports, including sailing and skiing. His goal was to buy his own sailboat and maybe one day, offer exclusive dinners on the boat.

Cassidy shared that her goal was to open an inn, hopefully at Crystal Lake in Lakeview, Maine. Peter had been to Lakeview years earlier with his parents. He loved the lake, the friendly little town and its close proximity to the coast.

Looking back on that time, Cassidy was sure there had been a little spark between her and Peter, but she was also coming off of heartbreak from her broken engagement from Ben and it didn't seem like a good idea to encourage any romantic feelings. Yet, she thought at the time there could be something between them in the future—maybe.

Before Cassidy left the spa that weekend, she told Peter if she ever opened her inn, she would absolutely call him to come be her chef. Peter said that he would absolutely say yes if she ever called and made the offer.

Several years later Cassidy made the call to Peter and as they say, the rest was history. Peter was able to join Cassidy at Crystal Lake Inn at the beginning of the kitchen renovations and his past experience was invaluable in helping to keep the project on track.

As for the little romantic spark Cassidy and Peter had felt several years earlier, they both knew it wasn't a good idea to get romantically involved since they worked so closely together. Yet, every so often, someone else would pick up on the closeness of their relationship and tease them about it.

Early on, even Amanda and Trish teased Cassidy about a possible romantic relationship between her and Peter, but over time it became clear they were more like brother and sister and that is how they both liked it.

On the flip side, Cassidy thought that maybe Amanda was interested in something deeper with Peter, but neither he nor Amanda ever made a move towards the other.

Since Peter had agreed to a long-term contract with the inn, Cassidy approached him about moving on-site. When the inn was renovated and expanded a few years ago, several rooms were built on the back of the inn. Both Cassidy and Peter had their own private entrance and living and sleeping quarters, with small kitchens and baths. There was also a guest suite between their rooms, which gave each of them even more privacy and also allowed them to have personal guests or friends and family stay with them. Their private suites could also be accessed from behind the office down a long hallway. This made it easy for them to always be available if needed yet have privacy when they wanted it.

"Before I go stow my suitcase away, do you want to give me an update on what disasters you've caused while I was away?"

"That may take a while but first, how is your mother? Still improving each day?"

"Yes. She's doing well, and my sister came yesterday to spend the week with her. Of course, she's already complaining that we are hovering too much. I doubt my sister will get to stay the entire week before Mom kicks her out. By the way, the flowers you sent her were beautiful and they put a big smile on her face. Thank you for thinking of her."

"Why don't you go get settled and then we can grab a cup of coffee and catch up. It's been an interesting couple of weeks and it's going to take some time to go over everything."

Peter was already headed down the hall as he yelled over his shoulder, "I'll meet you in the office in thirty minutes."

As luck would have it, when Cassidy went to check in with one of the part-time girls who helped at the front desk, there was a problem with a series of reservations. Cassidy had to help sort out the issues. By the time she was done and went to find Peter, he was already on the phone ordering food and supplies. The afternoon sped by and it wasn't until after the daily "Sit-n-Sip" that Cassidy and Peter were able to sit down and catch up.

"Okay, spill it. What's been going on around here? I heard a few rumblings of a lost rabbit and rambunctious twins or was it the other way around, lost twins, a rambunctious rabbit, and a new addition who already booked his room for next year?"

Cassidy almost spit out her coffee from laughing so hard. Thinking about the events of the past few weeks, including earlier that morning, she could see how bizarre things might sound if you only heard bits and pieces. She decided to give Peter the full play-by-play and not leave out any important details. Working backwards, she started with the newest addition: as she shared the picture of little John Connelly Jr, they both smiled and said "aww."

Cassidy especially enjoyed telling Peter about the extremely rude guest in Room #5.

"The guest in Room #5 couldn't really be that bad if he helped find the stuffed bear." Peter pretended to be dismayed at her and put his hands on his hips, shaking his head. "I think you and your gal-pals got what you deserved for eavesdropping. You know nothing good ever came from snooping. I can't wait to meet this guest. What's his name?"

"First of all, Baxter was a stuffed rabbit. Not a bear. Get your facts correct. We were not intentionally snooping, but we did hear some odd conversations and I take my responsibilities to protect our guests very seriously. If you had been here, I would have asked you to deal with Mr. Grumpy."

"Wait. You called the guest *Mr. Grumpy*? Don't you have a strict rule against calling any of our customers by pet names? You're breaking your own rules. He can't really be *that* bad." Now Peter was more amused than alarmed but feigned indignance. "Wait a minute... is there something you're not telling me?'"

"Not much. His reservation was vague. He requested a large suite that's private and quiet. He indicated he only wanted maid service when his DO NOT DISTURB sign wasn't on his door—which has been never. He's asked for a three-week rental with the option to extend another month if he's happy with his stay. He said he's here to work on a project and would be staying in his room most of the time. I already shared the strange conversations we overheard and how rude he was to me when I tried to serve him a meal. I will say that he was truly kind to help find Baxter and to keep the twins from getting hurt when they wandered away from their parents down by the lake. But then, he left the inn for a few days without any explanation."

"It's not that unusual for a guest to take a side trip while keeping their room with us. Many of our repeat guests use this as their home-base when they go on multi-day hiking tours or weekend trips to Boston or New York City. Why are you so irritated this time?"

"You don't understand. There is something *off* about this guy. It feels like he's hiding something. He's a late riser and I was cleaning up the breakfast buffet a few mornings ago when he stopped by the dining room. We had a pleasant conversation. He asked a lot of questions, but he avoided answering direct questions about his project or what brought him to stay at the inn."

Cassidy slightly hesitated and then continued, "even when we were outside searching for the missing stuffed rabbit, I felt like he was getting ready to tell me something but then he leaned forward and..." Cassidy realized that she had said too much and tried to backtrack by saying, "and, and, and we came back inside, and he hurried off to his room. I know he's hiding something. Also, there is something a little bit familiar about him, but I can't put my finger on it. I know I've seen those big baby blue eyes somewhere before."

"Baby blue eyes? You didn't mention that before. Are you now making a note of the eye color of all our guests?

Baby blue eyes…oh no! Cassidy, I'm starting to think there's more going on with Mr. Grumpy than just some odd behavior. Are you sure there isn't anything else you want to share with me?"

"Nope. That's it. There isn't anything else to tell."

"I'm too tired to argue with you tonight," Peter said as he tried to hide a big yawn. "It was a long drive this morning and I left my mother's house before daybreak so I could get back here to rescue you. Although, after speaking to a few of our guests, it sounded like everyone was enjoying their stay and a few even said the meals were delicious. I plan to really dial it up for breakfast in the morning. I'll show them what an incredibly good meal tastes like." And with that, Peter blew a kiss towards Cassidy and walked out of the office.

A few seconds later, Cassidy heard the door to Peter's private suite close. She was left with her thoughts, which quickly turned back to Jack and how hurt she felt. She still hadn't heard from him. She quickly reminded herself that she was done with him. He was just a normal guest and she planned to steer clear of him whenever possible.

She walked around the community room and dining room as she always did every night before retiring to her suite. Everything was in order. Nothing was out of place. *Nothing, that is, except for my heart*, she thought as she walked down the hallway and headed to bed.

CHAPTER 12

Other than the harsh overhead fluorescent lights and a few other lights in the hallways of the twentieth floor, the office building of Patterson Publishing was empty and dark. Jack was pacing along the long wall of windows that overlooked Park Avenue as Thornton walked the attorneys to the elevators after their meeting.

New York City never really slept at night. Beams of office lights could be seen in several of the buildings adjacent to Patterson Publishing, but most of the offices were dark and looked deserted. On the street below Jack could see a steady stream of yellow taxis, people hurrying along on the sidewalk, and the ever-present red and green from the long ribbon of traffic lights going down Park Avenue. Manhattan was his favorite part of the city.

Jack could see the cars and the people, but the only sounds he could hear were the hum of the air conditioning, the remote sound of the elevator doors closing and the clicking of heels hitting the tile floors. Jack knew that Thornton would be back any minute, so he started gathering his belongings and stuffed everything into his briefcase.

"How do you think that went?" Thornton threw out to Jack.

"After several years in this business I still find it baffling how the simplest clauses in a contract can cause us all so much grief. At the start of the meeting, it felt like a small war was brewing from the opposite side of the table, but as usual Thornton, your experience and ability to de-escalate potentially volatile situations pushed us in the right direction."

"It's in both of our interests to come to a win/win situation. I need to keep you happy if I have any hope of you finishing book three. Once you do, however, I want to start talking about the potential for another series."

"Thornton don't even go there. I'm still struggling to finish the last few chapters of this book. I can't even begin to think about a new series yet."

Jack snapped his briefcase shut and picked up his coat. "I'll be back in the morning to review the changes the lawyers are working on tonight. As soon as we are done, I need to leave to get back to my book. The long drive up here gave me time to work out a few more pages. I don't want to lose the momentum."

Thornton and Jack walked to the elevator and rode down to the lobby together. After confirming their nine o'clock start time the next morning, the two men said goodnight and went their separate ways.

Jack's condo was in an upscale area of Manhattan and his building catered to busy professionals. They offered a host of amenities that made life easier for residents that traveled or worked long days. Opening the door to his condo and walking into the foyer to turn on the lights always felt good to Jack. He knew his condo would be spotless, thanks to his housekeeper. He placed his briefcase on the desk that faced the ceiling to floor windows overlooking the city skyline. After looking at the view for a few minutes, Jack decided to call it a day. His head was spinning and the long drive from Lakeview added to his exhaustion.

Before heading to bed Jack had a few things he wanted to take care of, including putting his tuxedo into a garment bag and gathering up his dress shoes and other items he would need for the gala the following weekend. He was glad he thought to get his dress clothes so he didn't have to ask his concierge to do it for him. The building amenities were great, and he took full advantage of them. He told himself he should also stop by to say thank you to those folks before leaving in the morning.

After checking his emails and not finding anything of interest, Jack got into bed. His last thoughts before dozing off went back to Lakeview, outside on the walkway when he nearly kissed Cassidy. Was he ready for another relationship? Was Cassidy open to one? These were both excellent questions, yet ones he couldn't possibly solve tonight, so he turned off the light and instantly fell into a deep sleep.

"Jack, I'm glad you arrived a few minutes early. I hope you saw the new updates from the lawyers. Do you have any outstanding concerns?" Thornton asked.

"Nope. Everything looks in alignment with what we agreed to last night. I hope we can wrap this up quickly. Where's the coffee? I'll need a gallon to get moving this morning."

"Coffee service is on the buffet. Help yourself. By the way, once we are done with the business at hand, I have a few other items I'd like to discuss with you so don't dash out of the room."

"Okay Thornton, I'm all yours for another hour or two but then I have to get back on the road," Jack smiled but firmly responded to his publisher. Thornton was always trying to squeeze multiple topics into the shortest amount of conversational time as possible.

Thirty minutes later the lawyers were done and they left the room, leaving Jack and Thornton to talk about other business.

Jack turned to Thornton. "What else did you want to discuss with me this morning?"

Thornton slid a stack of Jack's latest bestseller across the table. "I need you to sign these for the charity auction. I need five for this auction and I want to keep another stack handy so I don't need to bother you each time I need more signed copies."

Jack signed the books and slid them back across the table. "What else do you want to discuss Thornton? I was serious last night about not wanting to start a conversation regarding another series yet. This last book has been difficult, and I need a break. Give me a few months and then we can talk about future work. Anyway, you might not even like the finished product of the current book. You should wait to see how you feel once you get the final chapters to review."

"I understand how you feel Jack and I'll stop bugging you about it for now. But before you leave, let's go over the plans for the upcoming gala. I just realized that you don't have the tickets or any of the details about the event. I don't even know where you are hiding so I have no idea how to make arrangements for a car service to get you to the event. It seems we are both missing big pieces of information about schedules and locations," Thornton said scratching his head. "Let me grab the tickets so I don't forget to give yours to you."

Thornton walked over to his briefcase and pulled out two tickets and gave one to Jack. "I know you didn't really want to attend this event and I appreciate it that you agreed to go. The charity is headed by one of my favorite people, Kate. I think you've heard me talk about her in the past. She and her husband chair the foundation of a small hospital in Maine and the work they do has made a tremendous impact on the town and the region. The current effort is going towards the addition of a specialized children's wing onto the hospital. It's a great cause Jack, so thanks again for attending."

Jack took the ticket and without looking at it slid it into his briefcase. "I guess I should know a little bit about the event and the charity. Who is this Kate person you mentioned?"

"Katherine Taylor Moore, known as Kate to her friends, was a friend of mine in college. She's now in her late fifties, but she still looks twenty years old to me, and is breathtakingly pretty with long brown hair and big brown eyes. I remember when I first met her…" the publisher got a dreamy, far-off look in his eyes. "…I can still see her walking along the courtyard near our dorms, usually running late for class, with a large stack of books in her arms and a long ponytail swaying in the wind behind her. But I learned to never underestimate her petite frame…years of dance classes and exercise kept her in excellent shape.

"We dated a few times, but mainly we hung out with a larger group of friends. At one point I had hoped Kate would see me as something more, but before that happened her heart was won over by someone else. They married right after graduation and had two girls. I kept in touch with Kate through the early years of her first marriage. She was so happy. Her life seemed perfect.

"Regrettably, Kate's first husband died when the girls were young. Kate was shattered and unprepared to be a single mother. Thankfully, Kate's mother moved in with them for a few years to help out. It was an extremely difficult time for Kate, and she basically cut herself off from most of her friends and gave up her community work. I really worried about her during that time but she refused help from any of the old gang. I didn't have any option except to step back and honor her wishes to be left alone." Thornton seemed lost in thought for a moment.

"Kate's mother was a wonderful woman," the publisher continued. "Everyone called her Grams. She was known for her philanthropic work and she pushed Kate to get involved in the community again. Her mother saw it as a way to help Kate deal with her grief while moving forward with her life."

Thornton paused for a moment and then continued, "It was the right course for Kate. She met her current husband when she joined the board at the local hospital. They had a whirlwind romance and Kate and Duncan have been married for over ten years. Duncan Moore is the CEO of the Moore Investment Firm with branches here in the city and in a small town in Maine. Kate and Duncan will be our hosts for the event. I think you are familiar with the firm. We have some of our investments with them and they've always done well by us."

"It sounds like you let a good one get away," Jack teased back at Thornton.

"Probably, but I think Kate found her second Prince Charming and I couldn't be happier for her. We've remained good friends and Kate made it clear to her husband early on in their relationship that I was like a brother to her so Duncan accepted me and never felt threatened by our close ties. They have a cabin, which some might call a chalet, in the mountains and I've joined them in the winter a few times for some skiing. A few years back we had a fun weekend with several of our old gang from college, various spouses and probably way too much wine."

"By the way, Kate thinks that everyone should have a fairytale romance and marriage so she's always trying to fix up her daughters," Thornton added, winking. "She did a good job with her youngest who is married and gave Kate her first grandchild that she spoils rotten. I think her name is Adelaide after Kate's mother. But she's now working on her older daughter, Cassandra, so don't be surprised if the table seating is arranged to have you seated next to her. Kate mentioned that she thought you looked handsome on the book jacket and she said she would consider it a personal favor if you would attend the gala. It sounded like a bit of match-making to me."

"Thornton, you know how I feel about being set up. It never goes well for either me or the woman. Under the circumstances I'm not sure I want to attend the event at this point. You should have been upfront with me about the situation."

"Look, I'm not sure there will be matchmaking. I just wanted to forewarn you to be prepared. I haven't seen Cassandra since the summer after her father died. When I attended her father's funeral, I promised to come back the following summer, which I did, but I only stayed for a few days. It was clear that Kate was still heavily grieving, so I thought it was best to let her be. She shared some family pictures over the years and her daughter has grown into a real beauty just like her mom. I seem to recall that Cassandra owns her own business, but I'm not sure. Anyway, Kate booked rooms for us at the local inn, which she said is comfortable and has all the amenities needed for the weekend. If you give me the address where you're currently staying, I'll have my secretary make all the arrangements for the car service and she'll be in touch with you on timing."

Jack pulled up his reservation email for the inn and read the address to Thornton. "I'm staying at the Crystal Lake Inn, 555 Main Street, Lakeview, Maine. It's about a five-hour drive from the city so I'm glad we have rooms for the night."

Thornton looked puzzled. "Did you say the inn is in Lakeview, Maine?"

"Yes, it was far enough away from the city that I hoped you wouldn't just show up on my doorstep. Thornton, why do you look so concerned?"

"Take a look at your ticket," Thornton said with a big smile growing on his face.

Jack opened his briefcase and took the ticket out. He read the information on the ticket. "Are you kidding me? This gala is for Lakeview Hospital. What are the odds of that happening?"

Both men were deep in thought for a few seconds and then it hit Jack.

"Wait a minute. When I was trying to find somewhere quiet to stay, the inn where I booked was the only one near the lake. Is the place Kate reserved for us called Crystal Lake Inn?"

It took a second for Thornton to pull up the email from Kate. "Yes, it is! You are already staying at Crystal Lake Inn? That's amazing! Kate's email says the site of the event and the inn are within two miles of each other and they are providing car service from the inn to the event. I can't believe the coincidence."

Both men scratched their heads and started to laugh, but suddenly Jack remembered something Cassidy had said to him the day they bumped heads in the dining room. She said her mother's name was Kate.

"Thornton, could Kate's daughter be the owner of the inn?"

"I'm not sure. What makes you ask?"

"The owner of the inn is named Cassidy. You know...Cassidy could be a shortened version of Cassandra." Jack rubbed his chin. "Wait a minute, these tickets say the hospital expansion fund is called the 'Fund for Addie'. Cassidy told me her maternal grandmother's name was Adelaide. There are too many coincidences going on. It's almost spooky."

Thornton was in deep thought for another minute and then he told Jack, "If this Cassidy is Cassandra, I'm a bit surprised that over the several weeks you've been at the inn she never put two and two together and asked if you knew me. Cassandra is aware that I'm an executive with Patterson Publishing and if the two of you talked about your books it would seem logical that she would make the connection."

Jack seemed a bit uncomfortable for a second and then said, "except for the fact that I registered under Jack Burnett and not Thomas J. Burnett and I might have failed to mention that I'm an author. I said I was there working on a project. I needed the peace and quiet, so it was best to be as incognito as possible.

"When I checked in, I saw several of my prior books on the bookshelves in the community room and I might have accidently misplaced them in the back of the storage drawers under the bookshelves," Jack continued. "So far, no one seems to have made the connection and it's allowed me to focus on the final chapters of the book. I know it seems a bit underhanded, but you should be happy that it's allowed me to make significant progress on my book. By the time the gala is here I should be done with the final draft and have it safely in your inbox."

"Oh boy, I don't see how this will go as smoothly as you seem to think. If Cassidy is Kate's daughter and if we all end up at the gala together, you know it's going to come out that you are a famous author, especially since your books are being offered at the silent auction. How do you think that will make Cassidy feel? It's a good thing she is just your landlord right now or else I think you might end up the first guest ever kicked out of the Crystal Lake Inn."

It finally hit Jack that he could be in some trouble. "First, let's get our facts straight. Thornton, can you call Kate and see if our assumptions are correct?"

Thornton walked across the office and pulled his mobile phone from his jacket pocket. He clicked on Kate's contact information. After a short pause Jack could hear Thornton speaking with Kate. He couldn't hear everything they were saying but from the smile on Thornton's face Jack assumed that Kate was confirming their assumptions.

"So, what did she say?" Jack asked. He was eager to find out if his Cassidy was also Kate's Cassandra. Well, he didn't mean *his* Cassidy, but the Cassidy who owned Crystal Lake Inn.

"To be concise, yes, yes, yes and yes. In other words, yes, Cassidy is Cassandra. Yes, Cassidy is the owner of Crystal Lake Inn. Yes, Cassidy is Kate's daughter. Yes, your ruse is about over." Thornton was now laughing. "Jack my friend, it seems you are indeed in a bad spot. As talented as you are at creating international intrigue stories, you shouldn't have an issue creating a way to get yourself out of your current bind. Devising interesting ways to get your characters out of the trouble they fall into should be as simple as writing a new chapter in a book. I'll leave it to you to figure this one out."

Thornton paused for a second and then added, "In the meantime, I asked Kate not to say anything to Cassidy. Not that you said Cassidy was anything more than your innkeeper, but I'm starting to feel like there is more to your story with her than you are sharing. I think you need to figure out how you are going to handle this and how best to approach Cassidy. Now, get out of here and back to Lakeview and clear up this mess you've created. I'm sure I'll hear fallout from Kate at some point."

Jack gathered up his briefcase and after the two spoke for a few minutes about logistics for the gala and some business related to the book, the author hurried out of the office and to the parking garage to get his car.

After stowing his stuff in the car, Jack sat for a few minutes to think over the situation that he created with Cassidy. It was clear that he had feelings for her, even if he wouldn't admit it out loud. He didn't really lie to her, but he wasn't totally honest either. How would she feel when she found out the truth?

As Jack pulled into the mid-morning traffic of the city his last thought before getting stuck in the typical gridlock was about Cassidy. After thinking it through Jack was sure that Cassidy would see the humor in it, and they could move on from there. Well…maybe she would be the slightest bit upset with him, but they could work it out. Okay, let's face it, Cassidy was going to be totally upset and most likely ask Jack to find somewhere else to stay.

Oh boy, he'd done it now. How was he going to work things out? Based on the traffic jam he now faced, he had several hours to devise a plan and find a way to make this right for everyone. For now, he had to focus on the snarled traffic and the dark clouds forming in the sky. It looked like he was about to run into some severe thunderstorms.

CHAPTER 13

Peter decided to go to the kitchen early the next morning. He'd had a good night's sleep and wanted to do a quick inventory before he started on the breakfast buffet. He had two inventory lists: one for the typical food used by the inn and one for the weekend of the gala. They had an inn full of VIPs for the gala weekend. The pressure would be on Peter to make sure the meals were exceptionally well planned and delicious. For events like the VIP Sunday Brunch, Peter turned to his signature dishes.

Peter and Cassidy decided months ago that they wanted to go all out on the brunch and Peter had finalized the menu while he was at his mother's house. He had emailed it to Cassidy, and they agreed on the menu, which included his famous Crab Cake Sliders, Oysters Rockefeller, Norwegian Smoked Sea Trout, a made-to-order omelet station, a carving station with New York Strip and Rack of Lamb, and a variety of veggies, breads and of course a tower of sweets, including Peter's famous homemade cinnamon buns.

It was a large and complex menu, but one Peter had done many times in the past for special occasions like weddings and other VIP weekends. It also helped that Cassidy hired extra help for the kitchen, dining room and guest services. Cassidy like to be free to oversee everything and spend time with her guests. Not to mention, when

Cassidy's mother was in attendance, Cassidy made sure everything was extra special, which reminded Peter to ask her about the florist order. They'd need more flowers than her garden could handle since, on these special weekends, Cassidy typically put large floral arrangements in all the common areas and smaller ones in the guest rooms.

Yep, it was going to be a roll-out-the-red-carpet type of event at Crystal Lake Inn.

After finishing the inventory, Peter was pleasantly surprised that their daily food items were so well stocked. He'd have to remember to thank Cassidy for making sure everything ran so smoothly while he was gone, at least on the food side of things. All he needed to order were the items for the special brunch. He could do that later in the day, but first it was time to get the daily breakfast buffet going.

Cassidy walked into the kitchen and grabbed a cup of coffee. After a quick hello she went into her office, which Peter thought was a bit odd. Typically, they used their early morning time to talk about the upcoming day and agree on plans for the following day's menu. Thinking back to the conversation they had the prior evening Peter wondered again if there was trouble brewing with Cassidy and Mr. Grumpy.

Several minutes later Cassidy breezed into the kitchen. "Peter, I forgot to mention that we have a young couple who likes an early breakfast of mainly protein so they can hit the trails. If you can get their items ready early, I'll be back in fifteen minutes to get their food. I just need to finish stocking the yogurt bar first." Cassidy was already pushing open the dining room door as she said the last word, avoiding any further conversation.

When Cassidy came back to grab the meals for the early risers, she mentioned to Peter that Amanda was coming in that day to help the housekeeping crew start on the deep cleaning she wanted done before their VIP weekend.

Peter remembered to ask Cassidy about the florist order, which she said had been finalized earlier that week. He also thanked her for keeping his pantry and food items so well stocked. Before he could even finish his sentence, Cassidy said she needed to go check on her guests, so he didn't have the opportunity to ask her any of the probing questions he had about the guest in Room #5.

Something was definitely going on with Cassidy. She just wasn't her typical self. Maybe it was all of the stress of the upcoming VIP weekend, but Peter thought it was something more.

He was happy to hear Amanda was coming in. If anyone knew what was going on with Cassidy it would be one of her best friends. He'd be sure to talk to her before he left to go sailing that afternoon.

It was going to be a gorgeous day for sailing, and he planned to take full advantage of it. Sailing was his passion and his job at the inn allowed him to indulge several afternoons per week during spring and summer and time to ski in the winter months. His job at the inn suited him perfectly and Cassidy always made him feel like an important part of the success of the inn.

Several hours later he was finishing up the last of the breakfast cleanup when Amanda walked into the room. He was always reminded of how strikingly beautiful Amanda was, especially when she was dressed so casually and with her sun-streaked hair in a ponytail high up on her head. For someone who grew up in a privileged world, you wouldn't know it to look at Amanda today. She had on old jeans, a housekeeping top, one of the famous Crystal Lake Inn aprons and several dark smudges across her left cheek that looked like dirt, which only drew more attention to her smoldering big hazel eyes.

Peter was still amazed that Amanda preferred to make her own way in life rather than work for her father who owned several large hotels across the globe. He remembered the day she showed up at the inn and told Cassidy that she was tired of playing hostess for her father. As long as he paid her way, she had to do as he said. But now she was a grown woman, and it was time she stood on her own two feet. She asked Cassidy for a job and a place to stay for a couple of months. Amanda took a room at the inn and offered to help with the housekeeping. Since Cassidy needed the help, she gladly agreed to Amanda's request but only if she paid her for her work.

Cassidy helped Amanda work through her issues with her father and suggested that Amanda offer her father a compromise which might work for both of them. A few months later she returned to the city to smooth things over with her father. After a tense initial meeting they finally agreed to the compromise. Amanda would help manage their family's charitable foundation—James Blake Charities, which focused on helping the homeless with job training and improving shelters by donating hotel furniture from room renovations—but only if she could do it from Lakeview, and only part-time. After standing firm on her refusal to come back to New York City or to work in the corporate office, her father finally agreed.

Two years later Amanda had made a home for herself in Lakeview. She bought a small condo in town, rented office space in a previously vacant storefront under her condo, hired two part-timers to help run the foundation and still continued to help Cassidy at the inn every opportunity she had. For some reason, getting dirty and cleaning up after guests, who were not always the neatest people in the world, seemed to help Amanda find the balance she needed to thrive.

The arrangement seemed to be working for all parties involved and Amanda's father even came to stay at the inn several times. Their relationship seemed to be back on track, although he never left the inn without suggesting that Amanda might be happier in the city. She always gave him a big hug and politely declined. She was happy where she was.

Forging her own way made her just that much more special to Peter, although he wasn't sure it was anything more than a high respect for her versus something more personal. Peter had known Amanda for years and so far, they had remained good friends—nothing more.

"Hi, Peter. It's been a hectic morning and I need a good cup of coffee. I'll just help myself." Amanda grabbed her mug and brought it over to the table at the edge of the kitchen.

"I just finished cleaning up from breakfast and I think I'll join you," Peter said from across the kitchen. He reached for his cup of coffee and sat down at the table with Amanda.

They both sipped their coffee and were comfortably quiet for a few minutes until Amanda asked about his mother. Peter gave the update on the great progress his mother was making, and they talked about a few other items related to the inn.

"Cassidy caught me up on what I missed while I was gone. It seems you and Trish, as usual, came to her rescue. I wanted to personally thank you for stepping in to help while I was with my mother. I'm not sure what we'd do without you two."

Amanda blushed slightly. She wasn't good at taking praise. "Thank you, Peter. I'm always happy to help. Cassidy has always been there for me, especially when my parents divorced and my mother decided to move to some remote island and drop out of my life. As far back as our college days she was there for me and for Trish, even though I was two years behind her in age. She's always treated me like an equal and I love her like the sister I never had."

Peter decided to push the conversation a bit, "Cassidy mentioned a few issues, mainly the day-to-day stuff we always deal with, but she also mentioned something about the guest in Room #5. What can you tell me?"

Hesitating a minute to gather her thoughts, Amanda said, "The guest in Room #5 asked for us to leave him alone. He never comes to breakfast with the other guests, and the day he arrived we had a sort of hectic morning and no one was at the front desk to check him in. His room wasn't ready, and he was not happy. When Cassidy tried to make it up to him by taking a special meal to his room, he refused the meal and only cracked open the door enough to yell at her that he did not want to be disturbed. I'll leave it at that since the rest is more conjecture on my part versus facts."

"Come on Amanda, I can tell there's more to this story. Spill it."

Even though guests never came into the kitchen, Amanda lowered her voice. She didn't want Cassidy to overhear her. She told Peter everything, including what they found in his room and what she and Trish overheard the guest say on the phone about getting rid of someone before he went into the airport.

"Cassidy also overheard a strange conversation and decided to do some snooping by following him to The Perk where he was meeting someone, but that didn't go very well and, in the end, Cassidy made a fool of herself. The worst part is we didn't learn anything else about the guest, except for the handcuffs and other weird things we found in his room. On the other hand, it seems he saved two small boys from getting hurt on the rocks near the lake, and he went out of his way to find a little boy's treasured stuff rabbit. Now we don't know if he's a hero or some type of spy. I've never even met him. I've told you everything I know."

"That is pretty much the same thing Cassidy told me," Peter commented. "I do agree with her that it would be highly unlikely that the guest is some sort of spy. It's more likely that people who peek at the personal belongings of guests and do a poor job of eavesdropping will also jump to incorrect conclusions." He peered at her, squinting his twinkling blue eyes over his coffee mug. "All three of you should know better. Snooping and eavesdropping are also strictly against Cassidy's own personnel rules."

138

Amanda started to say something but instead playfully shrugged off the comment.

Peter continued, "I was only gone two weeks. What would have happened if I were gone for a month? I knew I couldn't leave you girls alone without something going wrong. Oh…and then there was the matter of almost burning down my kitchen."

Amanda looked up in surprise. "You heard about that little mishap? It was really nothing. The ovens decided to take on a life of their own and the only casualties were some burnt eggs and croissants. We cleaned up the mess and the repairman fixed the problem. How did you find out about that, anyway?"

"I have my ways of knowing what happens at the inn even when I'm not here. As far as the guest in Room #5, I plan to keep my eye on him. I feel like Cassidy is still a bit uncomfortable. She acted rather odd when I pushed her for more details, mentioning his 'baby blue eyes." Peter noticed Amanda looked down into her coffee, averting her eyes at his last statement. "I feel like something happened when they were searching for the rabbit. Does any of that make sense to you?"

"Blue eyes? Hmmm," Amanda said coyly. "I seem to recall that Cassidy mentioned the guest in Room #5 had blue eyes. I don't recall in what context she mentioned it, but it did seem odd that she would recall the color of a guest's eyes." A serious look crossed her face. "I did hear about the fiasco with the missing stuffed rabbit, but I wasn't aware that Cassidy had anything to do with finding it. One of the guests, Mrs. Miller, mentioned the situation to me the next morning and she only mentioned that Mr. Burnett had found the rabbit. She was so thankful. It seems her son wouldn't go to sleep without his favorite rabbit and his crying was keeping everyone awake. I wonder why Cassidy didn't mention she helped him search for the rabbit? That is a bit odd."

Peter could see Amanda wasn't going to spill anything on her best friend and the infamous Mr. Burnett beyond potentially sorting out the odd conversations they overheard. If Cassidy hadn't told Amanda about helping Mr. Burnett search for the rabbit, what else hadn't she told her and Trish? It wasn't like Cassidy to keep secrets from them.

"Anyway, I've got to get back to the crew." Amanda sipped the last of her coffee and stood. "They're doing a great job and we might get done earlier than expected, but I need to check on the new linens Cassidy ordered for the VIP weekend."

Amanda took her cup to the sink and rinsed it out before putting it into the dishwasher. Peter walked over to the sink right behind her. As she turned around to walk away, he moved over to stand between her and the door. He hesitated for a second and then raised his hand toward her face.

Peter could feel the bolt of lightning that hit the air between the two of them and was sure she could too. Blue eyes locked on hazel. Peter was the first to break the connection, handing her a paper towel. "You might want to wipe those dirt smudges off your left cheek before you go back into the inn. We try to maintain high standards of cleanliness here at Crystal Lake." He grinned.

Amanda blushed. She took the paper towel and looked at her reflection in the stainless steel oven door and was embarrassed when she saw that not only was her hair a total mess, but she did indeed have two dirt smudges across her cheek. She carefully wiped them off.

"Thank you for the coffee and the warning about my appearance. I need to hurry back upstairs. See you later."

After Amanda left the kitchen, Peter stood at the sink and thought about their conversation. He felt like something had shifted between them, but he wasn't sure. What he was sure of was that Amanda had blushed at least two times in less than fifteen minutes and that was unusual for her. He was also sure that he really wanted to use his thumb to wipe away the smudges on her face but at the last second that felt too personal for some reason. In the past he would have reached over and wiped the dirt from her face and not thought twice about it.

Peter continued to think about Amanda. What if things were changing between them? Would that be such a bad thing? If they tried a romantic relationship and it didn't go well it could make working together very awkward for them and everyone else. On the other hand, if it went well—that was something he needed more time to think about. Right now, the sea was calling his name.

After changing out of his chef's uniform and checking his emails, Peter grabbed his backpack and headed towards the door. He suddenly stopped and walked over to his desk and picked up a book. His friend, a best-selling author, had mailed him an autographed copy of his latest book and he wanted to take it with him on the boat. When Peter mentioned to his friend that he thoroughly enjoyed reading the author's first novel in the series, his friend sent him his latest one. He couldn't wait to read it. Peter loved a good spy novel with lots of action and international intrigue. He was disappointed that he had failed to take it with him when he went to help his mother. Maybe today he'd get the chance to at least read a few chapters.

CHAPTER 14

"Hello Mom. I assume you're calling to make sure I got my dress for the gala back from the seamstress. Yes, I did, and it looks great. What else can I do for you this beautiful afternoon?" Cassidy loved her mother dearly, but Kate often hovered when she was stressed or worried about Cassidy for some reason.

"I'm so glad you were able to find a dress in that lovely new shop on Main Street. I wasn't sure if they would have the type of evening dress you were looking for and you kept putting off our shopping trip until it was too late to spend a few days shopping in New York City or Boston. Where does the time go these days?" Kate said a little breathlessly.

Kate was a bit nervous for not telling Cassidy about her conversation with Thornton Reed and the true identity of her guest. It didn't seem like a big thing at first, but then Thornton had asked her to keep it secret and she wanted to honor her promise. If Jack wanted to keep his identity quiet so he could finish his book, then she would play along. She just hoped that Cassidy wouldn't be too annoyed when she found out. He was just a guest at the inn after all. It wasn't like he was anyone special to Cassidy.

"Mom, are you still there?"

"Yes, dear. I'm still on the line. I just called to say that everything seems to be going smoothly leading up to the gala. The last-minute details always make me nervous, but the event planner we hired seems to have it all under control. I wanted to make sure that everything we planned for the VIP guests at the inn has been confirmed?"

"Yep."

"Cassidy, a one word response doesn't give me a lot of confidence. Would you mind elaborating a little more?"

"Yes, Mother. Everything is good on my end. Amanda is supervising the cleaning crews who are almost done with the deep cleaning. The new linens are washed, ironed and being placed on the beds as the current guests vacate their rooms. The florist confirmed that fresh flowers for the common areas and for each room will be delivered on Saturday morning. Peter is back and we confirmed the menu for the weekend. It sounds perfect, you'd love it. I think that covers everything."

Kate didn't respond right away so Cassidy continued, "was there anything else you expected me to say? Is there something wrong Mom? You seem distracted."

"Everything is fine Cassidy. I just have a lot going on and I'm trying to check off all the items on the list the event planner gave me. I want everything to go smoothly." Kate continued, "there is a lot riding on this gala. The funds are for such a good cause and if all goes well, I think we might hit our financial goal for the children's wing and the Neonatal Unit. I have my fingers crossed. I better go. I have a long list of calls to make."

"Mom?"

"Yes, Cassidy?" She heard her daughter's tone soften a bit, which made her smile.

"You know I love you and I greatly admire what you and Duncan are doing for the hospital, but I also want you to enjoy the gala on Saturday night. Take a deep breath and relax. It will all go according to plan. Everything you set your mind to turns out brilliantly. Don't start second guessing yourself. It will be an exciting and successful event." Kate was glad Cassidy couldn't see her wipe the tears from her eyes. She was so proud of her daughter, but sad that she might stand in the way of her own happiness.

After a few final comments about plans for the weekend they hung up. Cassidy was still a bit worried about her mother. It wasn't like Kate to get nervous about these events. She was such a pro at handling them. Cassidy hoped nothing else was going on. It felt like there was something her mother was reluctant to share. She'd have to keep a close eye on her mother's behavior on Saturday. Regrettably, due to Cassidy's agreement with her mother to personally be at the inn to greet all of their VIP guests, she wouldn't arrive at the gala until dinnertime.

Cassidy heard her name being called so she stepped out of her office and into the kitchen, where she saw Amanda standing. "Hi, Cassidy. We just finished the last of the cleaning and the crew is restocking the maid carts. Everything looks great. I've never seen the inn look so wonderful."

"Do you have a few minutes to sit down and enjoy a cup of coffee with me?" Cassidy asked.

"Sure, I did have a cup with Peter earlier, but I can always use more caffeine." Amanda filled another mug and sat with her friend at the kitchen table and the two spent a few minutes catching up, then their conversation turned to the gala.

"Amanda, Mom mentioned that your RSVP included a 'plus one'. You haven't mentioned who you're bringing. Anyone I know? Maybe the driver of the fancy car with New York plates I saw buzzing through town a couple of weeks ago?"

Amanda should have known that Cassidy was going to bring this up at some point, but she had hoped to avoid the discussion for a little longer.

"I guess I should just go ahead and tell you and get it over with. A few months ago, when I was in the city meeting with my father at the office, he introduced me to someone from his law department named Kenneth. We seemed to hit it off and got together every time I went to the city. We had dinner, went to a few plays and attended a few Foundation functions for my father. It was going really well. Did I mention Kenneth was good looking and a fantastic kisser?"

Cassidy was surprised that Amanda hadn't said anything about Kenneth to her and, as far as she knew, to Trish either.

Amanda continued, "Dad needed me to sign some 'urgent' papers, so he sent Kenneth here to get them signed. It seemed a bit odd that I needed to sign them in person. I think Dad was hoping Kenneth and I would become involved so I would be tempted to move back to the city. A few days after Kenneth came to Lakeview, I called him and asked him to be my guest at the gala. He said yes and I *thought* he was joining me this weekend."

"You thought he was joining you? That doesn't sound very positive." Cassidy didn't want to pry but they were typically open with each other. As a matter of fact, Trish, Amanda and Cassidy were like sisters and almost always shared everything.

"Well…Kenneth called me a couple of days ago and told me he resigned from my father's firm, and he broke it off with me. Apparently, Kenneth found a bigger fish to fry. It seems he was also dating the daughter of a CEO at a larger firm in New York. When he popped the question to the other woman, he was offered some high-level job in her father's firm. He was playing us both until he could decide which one of us would be the better meal ticket. It seems I lost."

"Oh, Amanda. Why didn't you tell us? I'm so sorry. Are you okay?" Cassidy's heart went out to her friend. "I don't even know this guy and I can tell you he wasn't good enough for you. Your Prince Charming is out there somewhere, and you'll find him. I'm sure of it."

"I know you're right, but it still stings and now I don't have a date for the gala. I know we'll all be busy helping your mother with a few things so maybe I can just sit at the table with you, Trish and Peter, if we actually have time to sit down."

"That should work. I'll ask mom to update the seating chart. Don't worry about it. I'll take care of it," Cassidy offered. "Thanks so much for all the extra work you've done these past few weeks. We just need to get through this VIP weekend without any issues and then you can go back to your normal life, and I can get out of spending so much time in the kitchen.

"It's so great to have Peter back," Cassidy added with a sigh. "With the VIP weekend I can't afford to burn down the kitchen and there's no way I can produce the elegant menu items Peter has on the VIP Sunday Brunch menu. He makes his job look so easy but after these past few weeks without him I can tell you it's not that simple."

Cassidy noticed that Amanda blushed when she talked about Peter. That was odd. They were all such good friends. Maybe she was still flushed from running around the inn all morning. On the other hand, maybe she needed to keep an eye on this situation. Was something brewing between Peter and Amanda?

Amanda got up to leave but Cassidy stopped her by saying, "Did you notice if Mr. Burnett was back in his room today? I haven't seen him." Cassidy tried to act nonchalant while asking her question.

"No, he wasn't in his room, but he still had some personal items in there, so I assumed he was returning. I heard Trish say he had to leave for some business reason, but he planned to come back yesterday. I guess he got delayed."

Amanda seemed to hesitate for a moment, then spoke up again. "Cassidy, you seem to be rather interested in Mr. Burnett's comings and goings. Are you still concerned about those crazy comments we thought we overheard? Looking back, I think Trish and I were letting our imaginations run away from us. You aren't worried, are you?"

Now Cassidy felt her face flush. She hadn't shared that she and Jack had almost kissed the night they found Baxter. She knew her friends could read her well, so she tried her best to look casual as she answered.

"Worried? No, I'm not worried about any of that spy stuff. I just wanted to determine if he's checking out or not. I did the VIP reservations around his room so he can extend his stay if he wants to, but I'd rather be sure, so I don't turn anyone else away unnecessarily."

"If Mr. Burnett doesn't return today, I think you should call him and ask him about his plans. It does seem a bit odd. By the way, I was looking at the bookings for the next month and I decided to check the ratings from our most recent guests. I saw that the Millers left a Five-Star rating and some comments about you and Mr. Burnett finding a missing rabbit. Is there more to the story that you want to share?"

Now Cassidy was on the hotseat. She wasn't sure there was anything more to tell. After the scene on the walkway, she was left disappointed and confused. It reminded her again that she felt a connection between them, and she had so hoped that he was going to kiss her. Why did he pull back? The only answer that Cassidy could come up with was that he didn't find her appealing, which hurt.

"Nope. Nothing exciting to share. The stuffed toy was lost. The twins were crying. The inn was in an uproar. Several guests helped search for the rabbit. The rabbit was found. End of story," Cassidy battled hard to keep her emotions from showing on her face, hoping she didn't sound too curt in the process.

To avoid any further questions along these lines Cassidy made a big show of looking at her watch. "It's time for me to get things ready for tonight's Sit-n-Sip. Are you going to hang around for a drink tonight?"

"I wish I could stay but I've got to run. I have to pick up my dress for the gala from the cleaners before they close at six o'clock. I plan to be here around ten o'clock tomorrow so I can get the crew ready to do the room change-overs and get the rest of those beautiful new linens on the beds. Thanks again for putting me and Trish up for the weekend. I'll bring my suitcase and things for the gala when I arrive in the morning. It's going to be a fun event, even if I am going stag."

"You'll have all of your friends around you, so you won't be alone," Cassidy added.

"By the way," Cassidy said as Amanda was walking out the door, "you know my mother and her continued efforts to fix me up. I assume there will be a last-minute seating change and some boring eligible bachelor added to our table. You never know. One of these days my mother's meddling might actually end up in adding someone interesting to our table."

"We can only hope," Amanda called over her shoulder as she left the inn.

Once Amanda left, the kitchen was way too quiet, so Cassidy turned on the radio Peter kept at his prep table. She tuned to an easy listening station and got to work baking her famous chocolate chip cookies, chopping veggies and preparing a spinach dip.

As she worked, her mind went back to her conflicted feelings about Jack. At first, she thought he was one of the rudest guests she ever had at the inn. That turned into concern that maybe he was into something sinister, which turned into believing he might be a good guy when he brought the Miller twins to safety off the rock by the lake. Then there was his rescue of the now-famous Mr. Baxter. Throw in the hug and almost kiss on the walkway, which was a big plus in the positive category. But then the big minus for standing her up without explanation.

Where did that leave her feelings? As Cassidy thought through how she felt, she went through the entire range of emotions, but she landed, yet again, on being hurt and mad. And that is where she left it for now.

Thirty minutes later Cassidy was wheeling the cart out to the porch and getting everything set up for the nightly Sit-n-Sip. Since a few guests were already on the porch Cassidy spent the next few minutes filling glasses and chatting with guests about their day. She loved this time of day as everyone was winding down for either a quiet night at the lake or dinner in town.

"Hello, beautiful."

Cassidy quickly turned around to see Peter walking across the porch, looking freshly showered, his hair still wet.

"Hey, Peter. How was sailing this afternoon?"

"It was fantastic. There was the right amount of wind to keep the sails filled, yet not so much that I had to work them. It was crowded at the marina, so I decided to go several miles out to one of the lesser known spots. Since only the locals know about it, I typically find it deserted in the middle of the day. I stopped there for a late lunch and a bit of reading. One of my old college buddies sent me his latest book and I wanted to read it in case he asked me if I liked it. It's a page turner for sure. I was genuinely enjoying it, but the warm sun and the motion of the boat lulled me into a nice nap just a few minutes into my reading."

"That's interesting. I have a new book a recent guest left for me. It's on the bestseller's list and I've tried to start it several times over the past few weeks but every time I pick it up something calls my attention away and I've yet to even get past the cover."

Just as Cassidy was going to mention the title of the book, she heard a crash and turned around to see that one of her guests had dropped his glass, which hit the floor and shattered. Cassidy kept a small broom and dustpan handy right inside the door in a coat closet. She quickly took care of the situation and gave her guest a new drink. All was well.

As she was walking back to Peter, a guest asked for dinner options in town. Giving her full focus to her guest,

Cassidy asked a few questions to confirm she was making the best recommendation. Deciding on the restaurant, Cassidy offered to quickly call and make the reservations for them. By the time she was finished and turned around to resume her conversation with Peter, she realized he had slipped away.

Cassidy frowned when she thought about that book. If she didn't know better, she might think that the book was bad luck. Every time she went to pick it up there was some sort of calamity. This time she only had to mention the book and a glass shattered. Maybe it was best to just put the book back on the bookshelf in the community room and leave it alone. She didn't need any other forces causing her trouble. She seemed to be finding enough trouble on her own these days.

A few hours later Cassidy took a final look around, as she always did, to make sure that everything was in order before she retired to her suite for the evening. She was such a creature of habit, but it felt good to double check. Making sure her guests had plenty of snacks and beverages helped to keep them happy and helped to keep her customer satisfaction ratings high.

Cassidy wasn't quite ready for bed, so she decided to take a walk up to the second floor. She always kept an extra supply of towels, linens and toiletries on the old-fashioned dresser that sat in an alcove off the hallway. She told herself that she wanted to double check to see if it was well-stocked so that her guests had everything they might need overnight—and that she wasn't looking to run into Jack.

Maybe she would just walk down to the other end of the hallway. She noticed the curtain wasn't hanging exactly right so she would straighten it. If she happened to pass by Room #5, it couldn't be helped. Again, she was thinking about her guests, right?

Looking around to see that no one was in the hallway, Cassidy walked over to Room #5. She looked down and no light was visible under the door. She walked closer to the door, but she didn't hear any sounds from inside. Cassidy heard footsteps on the stairs and quickly dashed back over to the dresser and looked busy. Who was coming up the stairs? She had mixed feelings about whether she wanted it to be Jack or not.

"Good evening, Cassidy," one of the other guests, a middle-aged woman, said to her.

Feeling somewhat disappointed, Cassidy asked if she needed anything and wished her a good night.

Quickly heading back downstairs Cassidy went straight to her suite. As she had said to Peter earlier, she didn't need a book causing her trouble. She got into enough of it on her own. It was time to put that book back on the bookshelf in the Community Room.

Once she got to her room, she moved the book off her nightstand and placed it on the little table by her door. It was going back to the bookshelf first thing tomorrow.

For now, she was going to bed. She needed a good night's sleep in preparation for the upcoming weekend. She got ready for bed and jumped under the covers. The last thing she remembered before she fell into a deep sleep was the scene on the walkway with Jack. But instead of Jack pushing her away she imagined him taking her in his arms and kissing her in a long and passionate kiss...

CHAPTER 15

The drive back from the city that normally took five hours ended up taking Jack more than seven hours. Not only was the traffic at a standstill when he left Patterson Publishing, a severe thunderstorm and several accidents along the interstate snarled traffic for hours.

At one point in Massachusetts, the backup was so bad that Jack decided to get off the interstate to refuel his car and grab a strong cup of coffee. He took the time to stretch his legs and let the fresh evening air energize him so he could stay awake and alert for the remainder of the drive back to Lakeview.

Seven hours later Jack pulled into a parking spot at Crystal Lake Inn. It was now well after midnight. He was so disappointed. It was way too late to seek out Cassidy. He knew he needed to explain why he left the inn so quickly, but he hoped that Cassidy was not too upset. He also hoped that between Trish giving her his update and the note he left for her in his room, Cassidy at least knew it was an urgent business matter.

Jack used his keycard to enter the lobby since the outside doors automatically locked at eleven o'clock. He was hoping to see Cassidy behind the front desk or in the community room, but he had no such luck. Jack headed upstairs to his bedroom.

Jack was wiped out and with the gala the following evening he knew he needed to get to bed, but first he wanted to hang up his tuxedo and grab a snack out of the basket the inn always kept stocked in each guest room.

Once he put his stuff away and grabbed his snack and a bottle of water, Jack sat in the chair near the window and gazed out at the beautiful full moon. From his vantage point he could see the large white orb shining on the lake, its reflection casting millions of lights like diamonds across the surface. It was a stunning scene. No sign of any storm clouds here in Lakeview like the ones he drove through on his way back from New York City.

Various thoughts were swirling through his mind. The stressful legal hassles he experienced over the past two days, the delay with finishing book three, and his growing feelings for Cassidy. On the other hand, there was good progress as the legal issues were put to bed and the book was almost finished. His feelings for Cassidy—that was the big storm clouding his thoughts. He didn't see blue skies for him and Cassidy, at least not yet. He needed time to sort that situation out.

He put his head back against the chair cushion and within minutes he fell asleep, only to wake up a few hours later; stiff and cold. He moved over to the bed, pulled back the covers, got comfortable and covered up. Again, in about two seconds he was sound asleep.

Jack woke up the next morning and knew that it was later than he had planned to rise. He could tell by the way the sun was already streaming in through the crack in the curtains. He had planned to get up early and go down to the dining room to get there before other guests arrived for breakfast. He really wanted to talk to Cassidy, and he needed to do it privately.

After quickly getting dressed Jack went downstairs and into the dining room. He didn't see Cassidy anywhere. He walked out of the dining room and over to the front desk. No Cassidy. The community room was also empty.

Feeling disappointed, Jack decided to grab some breakfast and coffee and wait for her to come into the dining room to clean up like he'd seen her do in the past. Smelling the food in the warming trays Jack realized how hungry he was. The food smelled great. He piled his plate high with a variety of different breakfast foods. Breakfast today seemed to be a bit more elaborate than in the past weeks. He assumed it was because some of the gala's VIP guests had arrived early.

Jack grabbed a local newspaper and sat down to eat his breakfast. He saw someone enter the room and his pulse quickened, but it wasn't Cassidy, Trish, or Amanda. Rather, it was someone else bussing the tables. *Darn.* Jack went back to his newspaper and his meal.

Three cups of coffee later and Jack admitted defeat. As he got up to leave the dining room a tall blonde-haired man in a white chef's coat and hat entered the room and was tending to the buffet line. The man had his back to Jack, but even so, he seemed familiar. Jack waited for him to turn around.

"Peter Cooper, is that you?" Jack couldn't believe his eyes. It was his old college roommate.

"Jack, what are you doing here at our quaint little inn?" Peter asked with a big smile forming across his face. "I can't believe it. We haven't seen each other in years, and we bump into each other in Lakeview. What are the odds of that?" Jack and Peter shook hands.

"I knew you left the boutique inn and spa, but I never knew where you ended up," Jack said. "Now that I've spent a few weeks in Lakeview, I can see why you're here. It's a beautiful place and I noticed all the large sailboats at the marina. I assume one of those is yours?"

"Yep. I love it here. Being the chef at Crystal Lake Inn allows me time to pursue all my passions—being a chef and plenty of time to sail and ski. My sailboat is over at the coastal marina. When the weather's good, I get to take it out at least once a week, maybe more. In the winter months the

SUSAN W. GREEN

inn is slower, and I get to spend time skiing and snowboarding. As you can imagine, we get a lot more snow in Maine than you do in New York City.

"I've actually been here for several years," Peter added. "I helped with the renovations under the new owner. As you said, Lakeview is a great little town. I can't imagine living anywhere else."

Peter stopped talking for a second and then said, "Hey, I thought you knew where I was living. You mailed me a signed copy of your last two books."

"I'm glad you got those. You know how it is, I sign the books, make a mailing list and someone else mails them. I didn't really take a close look at the return address on the card you sent me last year to congratulate me on bestseller number two. It meant a lot to me to get that message from you. You were always supportive of my writing career, even when it was going badly in the beginning."

Peter told Jack he remembered back to the end of their college days when Jack first started trying to find a publisher for his novel. Jack sent his story to a long list of potential publishers and several weeks later he'd started getting back big envelopes with a returned manuscript and a rejection letter. On many of those days the guys ended up at the local bar for a few drinks to drown their sorrows. He recalled the day only a letter came—no returned manuscript. Of course, good news also called for a trip to the local bar.

Soon after graduation Jack moved to New York City, found a great publisher and the rest was history. It was amazing to run into his friend again. Jack hoped they'd get time to catch up with each other.

"Peter, what did you think of book number two? I'm not sure it was better than number one, even though the critics thought it was. You always were an excellent judge of what would make for a good story."

"To be honest, I just started the latest book. My mom had an emergency appendectomy several weeks ago and I had to go help her. That's why I haven't been at the inn and

156

why we hadn't run into each other before now." Peter saw the look on Jack's face change slightly, like something had dawned on him, but he didn't say anything further.

"What just crossed your mind, Jack?"

"Don't get me wrong, breakfast has been great every morning, but I noticed the more elaborate options this morning and I thought it was tied to the VIPs staying here for the gala."

"I'll take that as a compliment, but you better not let the owner of the inn hear you say that. She might be offended." Peter smiled. "Due to the gala it's crazy around here today. I heard you mention it earlier, so I assume you're aware there's a big event in town tonight and many of the VIPs are guests at the inn. I'd love to catch up with you, but it will have to wait until late tomorrow afternoon. Will you still be here? I have a long list of things I have to attend to right now."

"It looks like we'll have plenty of time to catch up," Jack said as he got up to put his cup on the counter. "I'm not only staying for another few weeks, I'll also be at the gala tonight and the brunch tomorrow."

"How did you get invited to our little shing-ding?" Peter asked.

"Through my publisher, Thornton Reed."

"That's fantastic. After the brunch tomorrow, if the weather is good, we can sneak off to my sailboat and I'll really show you the beauty of the lake and the surrounding coastline."

Jack hesitated to say any more since he knew Peter was in a hurry, but he couldn't help himself. "I know you're busy, but you mentioned the owner of the inn, Cassidy...are you two...um...just friends?"

"Yes, why do you ask?"

Relief quickly flowed through Jack, and he chastised himself for feeling a little jealous of his friend.

"We seemed to have gotten off to a rough start, but then we got beyond that. I had asked her to have coffee with me in town at The Perk, but I got called away to New York City to meet with my publisher. It was an urgent matter. I sure hope she got the messages I left for her. I haven't been able to connect with her yet this morning."

It was like a bolt of lightning hit Peter, "Wait a minute. Are you in Room #5 by any chance?"

"Yes, why?"

"Oh boy do we need to talk. Sit down. I'll try to carve out a few minutes right now." Just as they started to sit someone came into the room and told Peter that a large delivery truck was waiting for him at the back door to the kitchen. The truck was blocking traffic, so he needed to go outside immediately.

Peter hurriedly got up and as he was leaving the room he turned towards Jack and said, "I have to get this delivery and then there are a thousand things I have to take care of before tonight. I'll try to catch up with you before dinner."

"Do you know where Cassidy is so I can speak with her?" Jack asked.

"She and her girlfriends left the inn a few minutes before you came downstairs. They were headed into town to the beauty salon. I don't expect her back for several hours. Sorry Jack, but I've got to run. I'll see you this evening," Peter yelled over his shoulder as he took off at a sprint.

Looking at his watch Jack saw that he had several hours before he needed to get ready for the gala. He had plenty of time to go to his room and work on his book or he could take a nice long walk around the lake, or he could sit in the community room and hope that Cassidy came back from her hair appointment so that he could speak with her.

While he was still going through the pros and cons of each option, he found himself in the community room, so he decided to grab the local newspaper sitting on the coffee table. Jack opened the paper and after several minutes of reading the same article over and over and still not comprehending what he had just read, he put down the paper. He didn't seem to be able to concentrate on anything.

Maybe a nice walk into town to visit The Perk would help him. Jack quickly ran up to his room to change into casual shoes and headed outside.

It was a beautiful late spring day with bright blue skies and not a cloud to be seen across the entire horizon. The temperatures were still in the low seventies—the perfect weather for a nice walk. Jack was halfway down the sidewalk in front of the inn when he saw a black limo pull up and stop. Mildly interested in who it was, Jack slowed down his pace. When he saw who exited the car he smiled.

"Hello, Thornton." Jack called to his publisher.

"Good morning, Jack. It looks like you were headed out," Thornton responded.

"Yep, I'm headed to the coffee shop in town. It's only a few blocks away. Would you like to join me?"

"I could use a good strong cup of coffee. Just let me check in and put my luggage in my room and I'll join you in five minutes. Is that okay? If you were in a hurry, you should go on without me. I don't want to hold you up."

"I have several hours to waste before getting ready for the gala, so I don't mind waiting." As soon as the words left Jack's mouth, he knew he had opened himself up for criticism from Thornton.

Thornton responded, "Jack, if you have time to waste shouldn't you be writing? Maybe it's a good thing I'm here so I can keep you on track. But I get it, if the creative juices are not flowing then it can be torture to sit behind a blank screen. I'll be right back, and we can go get that coffee. You are buying right?"

"Sure thing. I'm buying. Now, hurry up so we can take that walk."

Fifteen minutes later Jack and Thornton were already seated in one of the front-window seats of the coffee shop enjoying fresh baked croissants and coffee. After catching up on a few business-related items, Thornton asked Jack, "What did Cassidy say when you told her who you really were and about the connection between you, Kate, and I?"

Jack frowned. "I haven't been able to connect with Cassidy yet. The traffic was horrible last night so I didn't get back to the inn until well after midnight and I missed her this morning. I'm still hoping to speak with her before the gala tonight so she isn't totally caught off guard when my books and that terrible poster of me show up at the silent auction."

"I hope so too," Thornton said.

"To make matters worse, this morning I realized that the inn's chef is Peter Cooper, an old friend of mine. Peter has worked for Cassidy since she first renovated and opened the inn. I never made the connection with where he worked or with the town of Lakeview. There's no way that Cassidy will ever believe that I was totally unaware of all of the connections I have with her and the inn. The story is a bit unbelievable, even to me. Gosh, I feel a bit stupid also for never putting the pieces together. If I had, I would have registered with my full name and just asked Cassidy to keep my identity under wraps. I've made a pretty big mess of everything," Jack lamented.

"Jack, I'm getting the feeling that Cassidy is more than an innkeeper to you. It's been a long time since I've seen that gleam in your eye. While it makes me happy to see, I really think you need to tread lightly in how you handle this situation. I don't want to see either one of you get hurt. You can tell me it's none of my business, but do you know if Cassidy has feelings for you?"

Jack hesitated for a second before deciding to tell Thornton the truth. "I felt a spark between us on the night we were searching for a lost toy rabbit. We were outside and it was cloudy, so the lack of moonlight made the walkway very dark. When we finally found the rabbit, Cassidy was so excited she reached out and threw her arms around my neck and I returned the embrace. She leaned in towards me and I wanted to kiss her. I almost did when the thought crossed my mind that I didn't need any distractions and I harshly pulled away. I could tell she was disappointed. So yes, I think she also has feelings for me, but we haven't had the opportunity to explore it further. We keep missing each other. It's very frustrating." Jack felt regret fill his heart. *No time like the present,* he thought then, feeling caffeine and adrenaline kicking in and giving him a sense of urgency. "Let's head back to the inn. Maybe Cassidy already returned." Jack collected their trash and threw it in the trashcan, and they headed back down the sidewalk.

About three blocks from The Perk, Jack noticed the sign above one of the storefronts that said, Crystal Lake Salon and Spa. He wondered if Cassidy and her friends were inside. Jack pulled on Thornton's arm. "Slow down a bit, I want to casually look in the window of the Salon and Spa. Cassidy might be inside. If she's just sitting in a chair waiting to get her hair done, maybe I can coax her to come outside and speak with me. If she does, would you mind walking on ahead to give us some privacy?" Jack asked.

"No problem," Thornton replied with a smile on his face. "Jack, after you had sworn off women, this side of you is quite fascinating. Maybe Cassidy will be the one to finally win your heart. On the other hand…" Thornton scratched his head, "if this goes badly, I'll have Kate to deal with as well. This situation could mean trouble for both of us my friend. I guess it's worth the risk?"

Jack grinned, his rebellious side winning his internal debate and casting any remaining doubts aside. "You bet."

The Downtown Revitalization project had included the placement of sturdy benches on both sides of Main Street, along with a dozen or so large hanging baskets which were overflowing with flowers now that it was spring. Lucky for Jack, there was a bench in front of the salon window. Thornton sat down so he could enjoy Lakeview's renovated main street. On a gorgeous day like today, many of the merchants had placed small displays of merchandise and sale items on the sidewalk in front of their stores. Thornton could see that several store owners were also outside speaking to visitors and locals. Lakeview truly was one of America's small-town gems.

Jack walked up to the bench, but instead of sitting down, he put his foot up on the bench and pretended to be retying his sneaker while glancing into the salon's window. The bright sunlight was reflecting off the large window so it took a couple of seconds for Jack's eyes to refocus so he could see clearly inside.

When his vision cleared, he immediately locked eyes with Cassidy, who happened to be sitting in a chair facing the street and reading a magazine. Jack raised his hand to wave at her, but his hand stopped in mid-air. His attention was distracted by some type of tin foil sticking out in various directions all over her head. The sunlight was bouncing off the foil and the image he saw looked similar to the old black-and-white alien movies he'd seen on TV as a child. Jack was totally caught off-guard and took a step back, trying to determine what he was seeing.

When Cassidy saw that it was Jack staring at her through the window she froze. Realizing how she must look with dye on her hair, foil highlighting wraps sticking out from her scalp and a mud-moisturizing scrub of green goo on her face, she let out a very loud shriek. Her shriek could be heard all the way through the glass. Jack wasn't sure who was more stunned, him or Cassidy. The next sound he became aware of was Thornton laughing loudly as he stood behind Jack seeing the scene unfold.

Jack quickly looked away and immediately started walking at a fast pace away from the salon window. Now what had he done? He added another black mark against him in Cassidy's book. He couldn't get back to the safety of his room fast enough. He turned around and called to Thornton to get moving, but Jack didn't wait for his friend to catch up with him, alternatively jogging and speed-walking until he arrived back to the inn.

Meanwhile, back inside the salon, calamity ensued. When Cassidy realized that it was Jack looking at her through the salon window, she'd let out such a loud shriek that it scared one of the manicurists who jumped in surprise and painted a streak of dark red nail polish down the entire length of Amanda's thumb on her right hand. As if that wasn't bad enough, the shampoo girl got distracted trying to figure out who was screaming and accidently let the water sprayer drop into the sink, which caused the hose to take on a life of its own and sprayed water all over Trish's blouse and doused the shampoo girl from the top of her head to her waist.

It was pure chaos. When everyone got themselves under control, there were several moments of complete silence across the salon while everyone took stock of what had happened. The staff of the salon looked terrified by the situation, but Cassidy started to laugh and suddenly everyone was howling at the string of incidents caused by her shriek.

"I'm so sorry everyone. It seems my careless shriek started a domino effect. I owe each of you an apology," Cassidy finally was able to say.

Trish walked up to Cassidy and gave her a hug. "Don't worry about it. The smock helped protect my clothes, we put the shampoo girl under the hair dryer and the manicurist already has most of the red nail polish rubbed off of Amanda's finger. What made you shriek in the first place? Are you okay?"

"I was sitting by the window reading a magazine and I saw a movement from the corner of my eye. When I looked up it was...well, you'll never guess who it was," Cassidy trailed off her words.

"Oh no. It wasn't Mr. Burnett, was it?"

"Of *course* it was. What was he doing peeping into a women's hair salon window? That man will be the death of me. Something always goes wrong when he's involved. He goes from being rude and obnoxious to being a knight in shining armor by saving little boys and their toys to being a Peeping Tom. One minute he's standoffish and the next he almost kissed me and…."

"Wait a minute. He, *what?* He almost *kissed* you? When did that happen? Details, please?" Trish requested as she sat down next to Cassidy and started tapping her foot in a show of impatience.

Amanda saw the two friends excitedly whispering in their salon chairs and asked her manicurist to let her take a quick break so she could join them. She headed straight over and pulled up another chair. "Okay, you two, what's going on? Cassidy, why did you let out that awful shriek?"

Cassidy looked at her two best friends and knew she needed to tell them the entire sordid story. If not, they wouldn't leave her alone until she did.

She spent the next ten minutes telling them everything. She filled them in on what had happened at The Perk when she bumped into Jack's table, which they hadn't been able to see from their vantage point outside, to the almost-kiss on the walkway, to being stood up by Jack several days ago. When she stopped talking, she looked at her friends who were staring intently at her.

"What's wrong with you two? I told you everything," Cassidy sighed.

Trish spoke up first, "Cassidy, I haven't seen you this interested in anyone in a long time. It seems to me that you really like Jack. I'm a bit worried since we've all had some concerns about his reasons for being at the inn. On the other hand, he left you a note and he did try to contact you the day of your date at The Perk, but as I told you he got called away on an urgent business matter. I don't think you should consider that as him standing you up."

"Trish, did you say that Jack left me a note? I never got a note from him." Cassidy seemed confused.

"Yes," Trish added. "Jack said he was leaving you a note in his room…I'm sorry I guess in my rush to get to my shop to fix the plumbing problem I forgot to tell you. And since the DO NOT DISTURB sign was on his door, none of us ever saw it."

Then Amanda added, "I knew you were interested in him. I've never heard you call a guest by their eye color before. That says a lot."

Cassidy dropped her head so she didn't have to look her friends in the eyes. "Yes, maybe I do have feelings for Jack, but he made it clear that he wasn't interested. I have way too much going on right now to even think about all of this. It's been a rough several weeks; first with Peter being out, then several issues with the guests, including the scare with the Miller twins' adventures, the malfunctioning kitchen equipment and the extra activities for the VIP weekend— it's just too much to get my head around. If you add to all that our mysterious guest whom I can't decide if I trust or not, my ability to think clearly and be logical flew out the window days ago."

Shaking her head as if trying to clear her thoughts, Cassidy decided to end the current stream of conversation. Nothing was going to be resolved right now and they had bigger things to worry about. They needed to get through the VIP weekend first. Cassidy quickly diverted the conversation to a safer topic.

"Time is ticking ladies. We need to get finished here so we can get back to the inn and relieve the front desk clerk, make sure everything is running smoothly and be there for the crush of incoming VIP guests. Most of them are due to arrive in about two hours."

There's too much riding on this VIP weekend, Cassidy thought. *Jack and all of the headaches and heartache he brings can wait.* They needed to focus on the next few days. Besides, there would be time to sort all of this out once the gala was over. Or so she hoped.

Cassidy decided to focus all of her attention and energy on the VIP guest list and the gala. *At least I won't see him there,* she thought.

CHAPTER 16

A couple of hours later Cassidy, Trish and Amanda, along with Peter, were back at the inn putting the final touches on the special welcome preparations for their VIP guests. The inn was a hive of activity.

"I think these welcome baskets are the perfect gift for each of our VIP guests," Cassidy said without looking up as she retied the cheerful yellow bow on one of them. "Trish, your idea to add a few of the inn's logo items is not only a nice touch but it's a good marketing idea. Hopefully, people will use the mugs. They are very striking with the inn's logo and the lake hand-painted on them. It's free advertising in their homes and offices. We are so fortunate to have such talented local artisans like Sarah Jennings and others in Lakeview. I've sold so many mugs and aprons Sarah agreed to put us on automatic reorder. That will be one less item on my things-to-do-list."

With tablet in hand, Cassidy took a last-minute tour of the inn, checking off items as she went from floor to floor and room to room. Her final stop was the front porch, where she decided to sit down for five minutes to catch her breath and do one final inspection. The front porch looked fantastic and very welcoming.

As always, Cassidy was amazed at what her team could accomplish when they planned well and worked together.

The inn had never looked better. There were vases of fresh flowers everywhere, including on the front porch. To avoid a bottleneck in the small front lobby, attendants and luggage carts were lined up at the end of the front walkway. This left their guests unencumbered to check in and go straight to the Welcome Reception or to their rooms, where their luggage would soon appear.

Walking back into the lobby Cassidy's nose alerted her to something delicious so she headed into the dining room to see what Peter had on the warmers. A light fare had been set out, including a tray of freshly roasted bacon-wrapped shrimp with a light honey glaze and homemade cocktail sauce, along with an assortment of tea sandwiches, a fresh salad, a charcuterie board and little finger-sized pastries and desserts.

Just looking at the spread made Cassidy's stomach growl. She was dying to try one of the roasted shrimp and reached out to snag one when Peter walked into the room and smacked her hand.

"These are for the guests only," Peter scolded.

"I'm starving Peter. Just one. Pretty please."

"Come back into the kitchen with me. I knew the crew would be hungry, so I set up an entire buffet in the kitchen for the staff. I think Trish and Amanda already beat you to it so you'd better hurry before they eat it all. I had sandwiches earlier for the luggage and valet attendants and we set up a water and lemonade station on the front porch. No one should go hungry, and everyone will be well hydrated. Stop worrying Cassidy. I can see that look on your face. Come with me and we'll get you fed."

Cassidy and Peter walked into the kitchen, which was a bit crowded due to the extra kitchen staff they'd hired for the weekend. Trish and Amanda were sitting at the table with plates full of food, so Cassidy and Peter filled their plates and joined them.

It was quiet for a few minutes while everyone enjoyed the feast Peter had fixed for them.

Finally, Trish spoke up. "Cassidy, do you think we're ready for the VIP guests?"

"As ready as we can be. I can't thank all of you enough for your help. The inn looks beautiful…better than ever due to all the small touches you three suggested. As I did my final walkthrough, I was so impressed with what we've been able to accomplish. Working together as a team we can do anything we put our minds and hearts to. You are the best friends and business associates I could ever hope for—" Cassidy finished what she was saying because she could feel her emotions rising and the last thing she wanted to do was cry on such a happy day.

Peter finished his snack and went back to work while the three women ran through the afternoon schedule to figure out who was leaving for the gala at what time. Basically, the three would be working the check-in and lobby. Cassidy was in charge of personally greeting each guest while Amanda did the check-in and Trish would see everyone to their rooms.

All of the VIP guests except one couple were expected to arrive before five o'clock so that they had time to change and get to the gala venue in time to participate in the silent auction, which was scheduled to start at six-thirty, followed by dinner at seven-thirty. The band would be playing softly in the background during dinner and around nine o'clock things would get into full swing with dancing and a well-known trio of singers.

Amanda and Trish would leave the inn at six-forty-five. The last guests were scheduled to arrive around seven and once Cassidy got them checked into their room she would leave for the gala. She figured she should arrive just in time for dinner.

"Okay. Any questions ladies?" Cassidy asked.

Both of her friends shook their heads no and got up to put their dishes in the dishwasher. The three of them headed out to their agreed-upon stations to welcome the first of the guests to arrive.

SUSAN W. GREEN

Amanda was at the front desk looking at the computer screen. "Cassidy, did you know that one of our VIP guests checked in around eleven today? I wasn't aware that we had an early check-in. A Mr. Reed from New York City. He's in Room #4. I haven't seen anyone new in the lobby or dining room, so I guess he's in his room."

"I'll go check on him if you'd like," Trish offered.

"Yes, please." Cassidy said, giving a big smile to her friend. "You can take his welcome basket to him and see if he needs anything. Also, let him know that we have a lunch buffet in the dining room should he want something to tide him over until dinner. Did anyone else check in earlier?"

"Nope. That was it," Amanda relayed.

Hearing a noise outside, Cassidy walked over to the large picture window and looked outside. "I can see two cars pulling up to the valet area at the curb. I guess it's show time, ladies. Smile everyone, and fingers crossed that everything goes smoothly. And again, thank you in advance for everything you've already done and everything you will do to make this weekend a huge success. I love you both and couldn't do this without you." She gave them both a quick hug and stationed herself behind the front desk.

For the next several hours it was 'all hands on deck' as they said in the Navy. There was a constant stream of new guests arriving for check-in, luggage being hauled upstairs, buffet items being refilled and welcome baskets being distributed. Except for a little bump here or there, it all went as planned.

As the clock chimed five, Cassidy left her two friends at the front desk so that she could go to her suite and get ready. That would allow her to already be dressed so she could stay at the inn until the last possible minute to welcome the VIP stragglers and then hurry to the venue to arrive in time for the start of dinner.

Kate, Cassidy's mother, was scheduled to speak then and to announce if the silent auction reached its fundraising goal. Cassidy was so proud of her mother and how far she'd

170

come from those dark years just after her father died. In those days Kate could barely get out of bed some days, and yet, with the help of Grams she found her way to climb back out of the darkness that held her down for so long.

Once her mom got her footing back under her, nothing could stop her. Kate rejoined several of her former charities. Helping others seemed to be just what she needed to look toward the future. Either Grams or Kate were at every recital, school play and all the major important events in which Cassidy and her younger sister Jennifer were involved. Despite not having a father, the two girls had a wonderful childhood where they felt cared for and loved.

When Kate met Duncan Moore through her charity work, it was love at first sight and Cassidy couldn't have been happier for her mother. Duncan treated her mom like a queen and under his guidance and experience from owning his own investment firm, he taught Kate new ways to improve her personal investment habits. It also expanded her sphere of influence in fundraising for good causes. Adding a new children's wing to the hospital had been a labor of love for Kate. It was also very personal. She called the project, *Fund for Addie*, which reflected both her love for her first granddaughter and the respect for her mother, Adelaide Grace.

When Kate's first grandchild was born there had been complications and both Jennifer and her baby had been at risk. As good as the Lakeview Hospital was, they didn't have a specialty Neonatal Unit and had to fly Jennifer's baby to the larger Children's Hospital in Portland. The challenge of having her newly-born daughter hours away added to Jennifer's stress and her husband had to decide whether to stay with his wife or go to Portland to be with their new daughter. Kate stepped in to stay with Jennifer while her son-in-law went to Portland to be with her tiny granddaughter. It was a tense situation for several days.

Fortunately, everything worked out fine with both the newborn and mother. Jennifer was released from the hospital after a few days. Little Addie turned the corner a week later and came home soon afterwards. Now she was a normal and healthy one-year-old. Yet, the drama had taken its toll on the entire family.

If Lakeview had their own Neonatal Unit, it would have been more manageable for everyone involved. Kate vowed then and there that she would do everything in her power to have a world-class Neonatal Unit in Lakeview so that no other family had to go through those terrifying first few days like they had.

If everything went as Kate planned, after tonight's benefit, they would meet their overall financial goal and construction could start on the new unit.

At six o'clock sharp Cassidy was back downstairs as promised to relieve Trish and Amanda. As she walked down the final few steps, she cleared her throat loudly to get the attention of her friends.

"Oh my gosh!" Trish and Amanda said in unison.

"You look gorgeous," Trish told Cassidy. "That gown fits you just right...in all the right places. The teal color is great on you. I'm so glad you had them style your hair up off your shoulders. It makes your neck look longer and that diamond teardrop necklace your mother and Duncan gave you when you opened the inn is the perfect match."

Cassidy finished walking down the stairs, being careful not to catch the toe of her heels in the hem of her gown. While she loved the flowing long skirt of the gown, she was a bit nervous about tripping over the hem.

"I can't wait to see you both in your dresses, so go upstairs and get ready," Cassidy told them. "I can cover the desk and make sure our guests get into the limos we hired to take them the short ride to the gala venue."

"By the way, there was one tiny hiccup," Trish said. "When the limo for Mr. Reed arrived, the driver came inside and said that Mr. Reed and his guest had made their own arrangements. They left for the venue with Mr. Reed's driver. I wasn't aware that any guest had made their own transportation arrangements since that was a part of our package, but it all worked out fine and the driver took the next couple who was already waiting by that point."

Cassidy thought for a moment and asked, "Trish, didn't you take a welcome basket to Mr. Reed earlier? Did he mention that he was taking a date? His room was booked for one only."

"When I took the basket to his room the DO NOT DISTURB sign was on the door and I could hear the shower running so I left the basket right outside his door. I went back a little later to give it to him personally, but it wasn't there so I assumed he found it and took it inside. I knocked so I could welcome him and see if he needed anything, but there wasn't any answer. So no, I don't know if anyone else was in the room. It's possible that his date is someone local or maybe staying somewhere else." Trish finished her update.

Cassidy got busy at the desk and before she realized it, she heard footsteps on the stairs. When she looked up, she was mesmerized by two lovely women.

"WOW! You both look stunning. I can't get over how gorgeous you both are. You are going to take the breath away from all the men tonight for sure." Cassidy walked over to give her two best friends a big hug then stepped back to admire both women.

Trish had on a beautiful off-the-shoulder navy blue gown with an empire waist that accentuated her light blond hair and her tiny frame. The color of the dress made her blue eyes look even bigger if that was even possible. Trish's overall demeanor spoke of confidence and quiet, unstated dignity.

Amanda's gold shimmering gown showed off her best assets and made the sun-streaks in her light brown hair almost glow. Being the tallest of the group at almost five-foot-eight, her stiletto heels made it easy for her to see 'eye-to-eye' with most men. She really was a natural beauty and only used light makeup. Her friendly demeanor made her a hit at most parties, yet Amanda still had an innocence about her that belied her extensive travel and life experiences. No wonder her father liked to have her play hostess at his business functions, Cassidy thought.

"Hearts will be broken tonight, ladies," she told her friends. "I don't want you to be late so go on and get to the gala. I should be there just in time for dinner. I don't want to miss my mother's speech. Your limo is waiting. Have a fabulous night." Cassidy gently pushed the women to the door, but not before they had one more group hug.

The chiming of the grandfather clock told Cassidy that it was seven o'clock. Hopefully, her last VIP guests would be arriving any minute. They had called her right before Amanda and Trish came downstairs and said they were fifteen minutes away. If everything worked out as planned, the last guests would check in, quickly change into their evening attire and be at the venue in time to still get dinner.

Cassidy's plans were to check them in, get them settled and leave for the venue, hoping to get there by seven-thirty. She locked up the front desk, grabbed her wrap and purse and was ready for action. The ticking of the grandfather clock seemed to get slower and slower. Checking the clock on her computer confirmed the grandfather clock was correct. Time was slipping away. It looked like Cassidy would be late for dinner if the final guests didn't arrive in the next few minutes.

Finally, Cassidy saw headlights out front and went to the door to welcome her last guests. She quickly got them checked in and showed them to their room. She let them know that a driver would be waiting for them on the porch, and she had alerted the venue to keep their meals warm until they arrived. The guests thanked Cassidy for her kindness, and they rushed into their room to get ready.

As Cassidy was passing Room #5, she stopped for a second. She felt badly that Jack would be all alone at the inn other than the one staffer they had left to care for things. If she had thought about it sooner, she could have asked her mother if she could get one more ticket and she could have let Jack know that he was welcome to join the party. Thinking it through, she realized that the black-tie event wouldn't have been something Jack would have planned for in his wardrobe choices. *Better to leave things as they were at this point*, she thought.

Cassidy hurried out to the car waiting to rush her to the gala. As it was, she would be lucky to get there in time to hear her mother's speech.

When Cassidy approached the car, the driver came around to her side to open her door. Cassidy realized that the driver was Derrick Williams, who was also a member of the local Lakeview Police Department. "Hello Derrick. I didn't realize you also worked for the local limo company."

"Hi Cassidy. Yes, one of my best friends owns the company and I help him out when he has one of these big events and I'm not on duty. This might be my last gig with the limo company. As you know the Chief of Police is retiring soon and I'm being considered for the position. It's why I went back to Lakeview University to get my Master's in Criminal Justice Administration. Now it's a wait-and-see game between me and a guy over in Bar Harbor."

"I heard the Chief was retiring soon. I wish you all the best Derrick. I'll be rooting for you. Now, please put all that special driving training into motion. I'm running a bit late, and I need to get to the event as quickly as possible."

"Yes, madam. Since there isn't much traffic on Saturday night, I should have you there in five minutes."

As soon as she settled into the car, she pulled out her compact to check her hair and redo her lipstick. Pushing her compact back into the small evening purse her fingers hit her phone, which reminded her to send a short text to Trish and Amanda: *Running late but on my way. DO NOT*

LET MY MOTHER SWITCH DINNER SEATING ASSIGNMENT. See U soon. As soon as Cassidy hit send, she switched off her phone so that she didn't forget to do it once she got to the event. It would be her luck to get a call during her mother's speech. Double checking that the phone was off, she slipped it back in her purse.

True to his word, they arrived a few minutes later and Derrick quickly jumped out to help Cassidy out of the car. As she stepped out of the backseat the toe of her pointy high-heeled shoe lodged into the hem of her flowing gown and she was thrust forward. Derrick's quick actions prevented her from falling forward onto the sidewalk, but instead she ended up firmly against his broad chest. She hit against him so hard it almost took her breath away.

Looking up at Derrick's face, Cassidy remembered how good-looking he was and what a nice guy he'd been in high school. Didn't Trish have a big crush on him at one point? *I wonder why that relationship never went anywhere? Not that I want to play matchmaker like my mother always does, but I think I'll ask Trish if she's run into Officer Williams lately,* she thought, making a mental note.

Cassidy heard Derrick clear his throat, which brought her back to her senses. It took her another moment to get the toe of her shoe out of her hem and straighten herself out.

A bit breathlessly and totally embarrassed; Cassidy apologized for her clumsiness. "I'm so sorry. I should have been more careful. If you hadn't been standing there I would have fallen flat on my face. What a mess that would have been."

Derrick looked down at Cassidy with a friendly smile on his face and replied, "Well, with all those doctors inside at the gala, if you were going to fall, I don't think it would have been too hard to get them to run out here to take care of someone as pretty as you. As a matter of fact, I think there would be a scramble to see who could get here first. But I'm glad you're okay."

"Derrick Williams, I almost fall flat on my face and ruin the most expensive evening gown I've ever owned, and you are flirting with me!" As Cassidy saw that Derrick thought maybe he had said the wrong thing she smiled and quickly continued, "Thanks for the compliment and for saving me tonight. It seems that our local policemen are always ready to help a damsel in destress. I truly do appreciate it, and your compliments made me somewhat forget how embarrassed I am at my own clumsiness. Thanks again."

"Be careful Ms. Taylor and have a wonderful evening. One of the other drivers will be here to return you to the inn when you call us after the event. I go on duty later this evening." And with that, Derrick saluted her, got back in the car, and drove off.

It took a minute for Cassidy to realize she was just standing on the sidewalk watching the limo drive away when she really should be hurrying to get inside. She promised her mother she would be seated at her table in time to hear her speech.

As Cassidy hurried inside her last thought before getting to her table was her hope that her mother hadn't done another switch with her dinner companion this year. If it all worked out like she hoped, she would be sitting in between Trish, Amanda and Peter. She was looking forward to a drama free evening with her family and best friends.

CHAPTER 17

Stopping outside the ballroom to collect her table number Cassidy was happy to see only a couple of seating cards left on the table. She knew that meant that the event had a strong turnout, which was good news for her mother and the foundation fund.

"Hi, Cassidy," one of the organizers called from the other end of the table. "We were expecting you. Kate stopped by the table to see if you had checked in right before she entered the ballroom. She explained you were at the inn waiting on the last of the VIP guests. You should hurry inside. I think they're getting ready to start."

"Thank you. One quick question. How did the silent auction and donation effort go? Do you think you are close to your goal?"

The young attendant's face broke into a huge smile, "You should hurry inside. I think your mother has an update."

Cassidy could hear the noise level of conversation in the large ballroom get quiet as she opened the door and stepped inside, just to the left of the last row of tables. She quickly took in the gorgeous room—the large sparkling chandeliers hanging from the ceiling, shimmering gold curtains outlining the stage at the front of the room, and flower arrangements on each table all set off by tall, tapered candles flickering on each. The ballroom took on a magical quality. She immediately noticed her mother heading towards the center of the stage. Cassidy's stepfather, Duncan, was already standing next to the microphone waiting for Kate.

"Tonight is the culmination of a tremendous amount of work by hundreds of dedicated volunteers across the past few years. When we started our vision of a Neonatal Unit for the Lakeview Hospital, we knew that our goals were lofty, and it would take a miracle to fulfill our dreams. We also knew that the generosity of the people and businesses of Lakeview and the surrounding counties would help us achieve this important goal," Kate took a breath and paused for effect.

"As most of you know, this new unit is not only a critical addition to our hospital, but it's also personal for me. When our daughter, Jennifer, delivered our first grandchild, there were complications and the baby had to be flown to Portland for specialized care in their Neonatal Unit. Thanks to God and to the talented staff of the hospital, little Addie is now a happy and totally healthy little girl."

Kate paused to help build up to the exciting news. "I can't tell you how excited I am to say that with the proceeds of all of our fundraising efforts and especially the money from tonight's silent auction, we've exceeded our goal! Our dreams will now become a reality!" Kate stopped speaking because the roar of the applause was so loud, and she felt close to tears. She hugged her husband and turned the microphone back over to Duncan.

"With full hearts I want to say thank you to everyone who made this dream a reality. Without further ado, please enjoy your dinner. We hope you all stay with us for dancing and our special trio of guest singers at nine o'clock. Have a wonderful evening," Duncan finished and headed to the table to join his party for dinner.

Tears were burning in Cassidy's eyes as she still stood inside the ballroom doors. She was always proud of the charitable work her mother did, but tonight, she was absolutely honored to call Katherine Taylor Moore her mother. Her emotions were threatening to spill over. She needed to give her mom a great big hug, but as she headed towards her mother's table the throng of people around it was just too thick for her to even get close. Cassidy was starving so she decided to find her table and come back later to congratulate her mother. She looked down at the card with her table assignment written on it and saw that she was at table #5. She headed across the room in that direction.

Several people stopped Cassidy along the way, so it took her a few minutes to get to her table, where several people were standing behind those already seated. It was hard to tell if her mother had pulled a fast one with the seating assignments or if she was seated next to Trish and Amanda, but either way she was going to push her way through the crowd so she could enjoy her meal.

As Cassidy excused herself around the last couple of people standing in the aisle next to her seat, she saw the empty chair at the table and smiled when she noticed that Trish was seated to her left. She hurriedly pulled out her chair and sat down with a thud. She immediately reached for her water glass to quench her thirst and at the same time looked around the table and was relieved to find she was seated in the chair next to Trish, who was seated next to Amanda and Peter. Yes, she was with her friends. Tonight was going to be a good night.

Cassidy started to say something to Trish when she caught the strange looks on the faces of all three of her friends. "What's wrong with you three? It's a great night! The gala is a success, all of our VIPs got checked in, the last ones to arrive just got seated, and I plan on having a relaxing and enjoyable evening. Stop staring at me. Do I have something on my face?"

Trish leaned over to Cassidy and whispered in her ear, "Room #5 is on your right."

It took a second for Cassidy to understand what Trish was trying to tell her and then it hit her full force. Her friends watched as the color drained out of Cassidy's face. She was terrified to look at the place card to her right, so she sat frozen, staring straight ahead.

Before Cassidy could even sort through her thoughts, she felt a hand on her shoulder and heard her mother's voice, "Cassidy, I'm so excited about reaching our goal. I'm so sorry that you were not here for the silent auction. Thomas J. Burnett's personally signed books and an extremely generous donation from Patterson Publishing put us over the top. It was all so exciting. Oh, let me introduce you to your dinner partner, Thomas J. Burnett. Thomas, this is my daughter Cassidy Taylor. I think you are staying at her inn. Have you two met?"

Cassidy started to choke on the big gulp of water she had taken and felt several people pounding on her back. "I'm okay, thank you," Cassidy said once she could catch her breath.

Standing up and turning around, Cassidy found herself staring straight into the baby blue eyes of the guest in Room #5. He stepped forward and shook her hand, both of them speechless for a moment. Cassidy was more than confused. "Mother, this man is Jack Burnett, not the author Thomas Burnett. There must be some sort of confusion since they have the same last name."

Cassidy saw the color drain from Jack's face. Clearing his throat, he finally spoke up. "I know it's all a bit confusing, but I can explain. You see, I needed total peace and quiet so I could finish the last couple of chapters of my current book, which is overdue. My publisher, Thornton Reed from Patterson Publishing, ordered me to find a quiet place to finish it or my contract would be in jeopardy. Thomas Jack Burnett is my legal name, but I've always gone by Jack so that's what I made my reservation under.

"Peter can vouch for my identity as we were college roommates. My publisher, Thornton Reed, is here also if, uh, you need more references. There's also a picture of me on the back jacket of my books." Jack gave her a sheepish grin.

Cassidy's head was spinning. It seemed everyone knew the true identity of Jack except for her. Thinking through her escapades in eavesdropping at his door, the fiasco at The Perk, the almost-kiss on the walkway, the shriek at the salon…Cassidy suddenly realized that she had made a major fool of herself. She saw the big grin on Jack's face and thought that he was laughing at her.

Totally embarrassed and humiliated, Cassidy rose from the table, but with her mind still whirling, she seemed frozen to the spot.

Jack reached out and put his hand on her arm, "Cassidy, I'm not sure why you look so furious right now. It was just a bit of confusion that is now all sorted out. Let's sit down and enjoy our dinner."

Peter walked over to Cassidy and quietly said, "Cassidy, I've known Jack since college. I just realized this morning that he was one of our VIP guests. We were all so busy today and I never got the chance to explain. Jack is truly a good guy. When I saw he was sitting at our table I thought we'd all have a chance to clear things up before dinner, but then you arrived late."

Cassidy was so overwhelmed that she couldn't think straight. What hurt the most was that Jack didn't think he could trust her with his true identity. Realizing that she was about to burst into tears, Cassidy quickly turned and ran from the room.

Behind her, Cassidy could hear people calling her name, but she couldn't seem to stop running. She had to get out of the room before she broke down in tears. She burst through the ballroom doors. A few steps outside the ballroom a pair of strong hands brought her to a stop.

Whirling around to see who was preventing her from getting outside and into a waiting limo, she saw Jack…or Thomas…or whoever he really was. She tried to yank her arms away, but his hold was firm.

"Cassidy, I'm not sure why you're so upset? Can we sit down over there on that sofa and talk about this?" He pointed to a sitting area off of the huge ballroom lobby. "Please."

Cassidy stopped straining to pull away and walked the few feet to where Jack had motioned and sat down on one of the sofas, as far away from him as she could get. "Ok, talk away, Mr. Burnett."

"When I first checked into the inn, I was under a lot of pressure to finish the last book of a three-book deal. I was told my contract was in jeopardy. My first two books hit the best seller's list immediately, which *should* be a good thing, but the notoriety and public appearances caused me to get off track with my deadlines. Then the added pressure turned into the most serious case of writer's block I've ever had."

Jack continued, "I was basically exiled out of the city to a quiet place and your inn seemed to be the perfect spot. I needed to keep a low profile and to avoid distractions. Once I met you, well, you became a different kind of distraction. Couldn't you tell I was attracted to you? I tried to ignore you hoping it would fade, but even when I wasn't with you in person, you were monopolizing my thoughts."

Cassidy felt her heart leap but was still flustered. "You're attracted to me? How was I supposed to know that? You were too revolted to kiss me on the walkway when we found the stuffed rabbit and then you stood me up at The Perk. What was I to think Jack?"

"I was *not* revolted by you. I wanted to kiss you so badly that night, but I kept hearing Thornton's voice in my head warning me against any distractions. I'm sorry about the date at The Perk. I was called back to the city for a serious contract issue. I told Trish to let you know and I left you a note in my room."

"I never saw your note and only recently found out that you actually left one because you left the DO NOT DISTURB sign on your door all the time, so we hadn't gone in there for days. When Trish told me you left, I assumed you decided against the date, and you found a reason to leave for a few days to let things cool down between us. Even if your version of events is true, what about the covert conversations we overheard about getting rid of someone before they got on the plane and the handcuffs and other strange things in your room?"

Jack burst out laughing. "How do you know about those things in my room and what I was saying on the phone? Didn't your mother ever teach you that no good comes from eavesdropping, Cassidy?"

"Yes, she did, but sometimes you can't help but hear and see things. You still haven't explained yourself."

"Cassidy, come with me for a minute." Jack offered his hand and helped her to her feet.

"Where are we going? I'm not sure I want to go anywhere with you," Cassidy said, even though she was starting to calm down and was no longer quite as angry.

"Just down the hall."

They walked in silence for the brief moment it took to get to the room where the auction had been held. As they entered, a couple of workers were still inside placing items in boxes and adding shipping labels.

One of the workers walked over to Jack and Cassidy asking if he could help them. Jack replied, "I'm Thomas J. Burnett, several of my books were auctioned off tonight. I was wondering, if you have yet to pack them, could I show one to my friend Cassidy?"

"Of course, Mr. Burnett. They are right over here."

Jack thanked the young man. He took Cassidy's arm and directed her toward the table the young attendant had pointed out. When they got to a stack of hardback books, Jack picked up the one on the top of the pile and turned it over to the back jacket. "I think this is a fairly good likeness of me, do you agree?"

The photo made Jack look even more handsome than in person if that was possible. There were those same baby blue eyes and now it clicked where she'd seen them before.

"Yes, I get it. It's you. Okay, I understand now that Thomas J. and Jack Burnett are the same person. That still doesn't explain the covert conversations and strange items you carry in your baggage."

Jack turned the book over to the front cover and handed the book to Cassidy. "Please read the bold print across the top of the front cover."

Cassidy took the book and while she still wasn't sure how this was going to explain the strange situation, she did as he requested. As soon as she read the words printed in bold lettering, she closed her eyes.

"Do you want to read it out loud, Cassidy, so there's no room for further confusion?"

"*Thomas J. Burnett, Best Selling Author of International Spy Novels,*" Cassidy read. After realizing it did, in fact, explain everything, she felt her face flush with embarrassment and shame. "I feel so stupid Jack. Can you ever forgive me?"

Jack reached over and took the book from Cassidy's hand and placed it back on the table. He then reached for her arm and lead her out of the room. He wanted to find a quiet place to show her that all was forgiven. Jack also wanted to show Cassidy exactly how he felt about her. Now that he'd sorted out his own feelings it was clear that he was falling fast for this wonderful woman.

They walked back down the hallway to the same sofa. Jack looked around and didn't see anyone else. He reached out and pulled Cassidy towards him but as she stepped forward, as luck would have it, the pointy toe of her high heal stuck in the front hem of her gown again. She lost her balance which made her stumble into Jack's chest. Jack tried to steady them both, but the momentum made him lose his balance and they both fell backwards.

Luckily, the sofa broke their fall, although Cassidy was basically laying on top of Jack with her dress up to her knees. One of her shoes had flicked off her foot and slid across the floor. Before they could get up and straighten themselves out, they heard laughter.

Looking up Cassidy saw several familiar faces staring down at them. Peter was the first to speak. "I suggest you two get a room. I think Cassidy has an inn full of them."

Peter's comment brought another round of laughter from the group. Cassidy and Jack looked at each other and then at the scene they'd created. They both quickly straightened up and started to laugh along with their friends.

"This has been the most interesting evening I've had in a long time," Jack said once he caught his breath from laughing so hard. "I think Cassidy and I have sorted out a few things, including confirming my identity. The fact that I write international spy novels hopefully explains the covert sounding conversations and the rather strange things you ladies found in my room."

Trish spoke up first, "Yes, Peter explained all of this to us while you two were, umm, well, doing whatever it was you were doing before we came to find you. We wanted to make sure that you two didn't kill each other."

"We almost did," Cassidy said. "Basically, I tripped and…"

"That's okay, no explanation needed," Peter said. Suddenly they could hear music and singing coming from the ballroom.

Cassidy was a bit surprised when Peter whispered to Amanda, "Would you like to dance, Ms. Blake?"

With the biggest smile any of her friends had ever seen on Amanda's face she said, "Why yes, Mr. Cooper, I would like to dance with you. Let's go back into the ballroom."

Amanda turned around to face the others and said, "I suggest we all return to the party and enjoy the rest of our evening." And with that, Amanda and Peter quickly turned around and headed back to the ballroom leaving Trish and Cassidy staring at each other.

Jack was a bit confused. "Why are you two staring at each other? Is it odd for Peter and Amanda to dance together? I thought you were all friends. You must have danced together in the past?"

"Yes, we've all danced together, and Peter has been our shared date many times, but the look on their faces just now was something else entirely," Cassidy explained. "We'll have to delve into this new development later."

"Trish, would you mind giving Cassidy and me a few minutes alone?" Jack asked. "I promise I won't keep her long. I have plans to dance with her all night long. But I was interrupted a bit ago and I didn't have a chance to finish what I wanted to say to her."

"No problem, consider me gone." With that, Trish flew back into the ballroom leaving Jack and Cassidy alone in the hallway.

Jack pulled Cassidy close. He slowly lifted her chin up and lightly brushed his lips against hers. Cassidy was so startled that she slightly jumped back, but Jack was quick to pull her back into his embrace. Once she realized he was going to kiss her again, she closed her eyes and leaned in.

She could smell his woodsy aftershave and feel the heat of his body next to hers. She wanted to stay right there in that moment forever. She felt her pulse quicken as Jack pulled her closer and kissed her again. This time the kiss deepened. She heard a soft groan escape and realized it was her own but didn't care although she thought maybe Peter was right, they should get a room. Before she was ready for it to end, Jack eased his lips off hers and put a little space between then.

Coming to her senses, Cassidy asked, "Didn't you tell Trish you had something else you wanted to say to me?"

Jack smiled, "That *is* what I wanted to say to you. That kiss. I thought that would help confirm how I feel about you, Cassidy. It seems in only a few short weeks, I'm hooked. That last kiss should prove it."

He continued, "I think we should go back into the ballroom and dance the night away. Or we could take Peter's advice and go back to the inn and 'get a room'."

Before Cassidy had time to respond, Jack decided for both of them. "Cassidy, let's turn this entire strange and unusual situation into a magical evening." Extending his hand, he asked, "Can I have this dance Ms. Taylor?"

"Yes, Mr. Burnett. You can have this dance and all the dances on my dance card tonight."

Jack took Cassidy's arm and led her back into the ballroom and onto the dance floor where they saw Peter and Amanda slow-dancing together. Trish was dancing with another friend of theirs from Lakeview. Cassidy also saw her mother and Duncan dancing. Her mother smiled over at her and did a thumbs up behind Duncan's back.

After their first dance, Cassidy was able to finally eat a few bites of the delicious dinner that had been re-warmed while Jack talked about how beautiful she looked, and they caught up a bit more. Then they danced for hours. It was a magical evening and Cassidy never wanted it to end. The music was perfect, the ballroom glittered with thousands of twinkling white lights, and she was in Jack's arms. She knew she still needed to sort through her feelings for him. She also needed to consider the fact that he lived in New York City, not Lakeview, and they'd have some distance to overcome. All of that could wait until tomorrow though because she couldn't think straight tonight.

Tonight was the most wonderful night of her life and she was going to enjoy every last minute of it. And that she did. In Jack's arms Cassidy felt safe, secure and loved.

CHAPTER 18

Hours later Cassidy lay in her bed. Her body was tired—
oh so tired—but her mind was wide awake. Knowing she
had to be up in a couple of hours she tried to clear her head
and go to sleep, but sleep was elusive.

Cassidy replayed the evening over and over again in her
mind, especially the parts where Jack was kissing her and
hugging her tightly to his chest. After the gala had ended
and all the VIP guests were transported back to the inn, Jack
and Cassidy sat on the swing on the front porch and talked
for hours.

When they finally stood up and forced themselves to
part, Jack took Cassidy in his arms one last time and gave
her a kiss so long and so passionate that she thought her
knees would buckle out from underneath her. Even now,
she could still feel the pressure of his lips on hers.

Cassidy tossed and turned for a few more minutes and
then she pulled another pillow across the bed and hugged it
close to her. One last thought of Jack and his dreamy baby
blue eyes and Cassidy finally fell into a peaceful sleep.

Upstairs in Room #5, Jack was having similar trouble
getting any rest. At least he could sleep in a bit later than
Cassidy in the morning. On the other hand, if he got up

early enough, maybe he could sneak into the kitchen and steal a few more kisses from her before the special brunch.

Then he remembered that he had promised to wait until after the VIP guests left. They would meet at the Sit-n-Sip. Finally, he calmed his mind enough to feel himself falling asleep. His last thought was how wonderful it felt to hold Cassidy in his arms.

Jack realized they would have several hurdles to overcome, like any new relationship. If he was honest with himself, he had never felt this way about any woman in the past. Cassidy was special and he was going to be sure he didn't mess this up.

"Good morning, Cassidy," Peter called from across the kitchen. "Did you get any sleep last night?

"I could ask you the same thing," Cassidy replied with a sly grin on her face.

"Whatever do you mean?" Peter innocently raised his eyebrows.

"I saw the shift in your relationship with Amanda. You can't hide that from me. By the way, I'm in favor of it, if you want my opinion."

"Thanks, Cassidy. Yes, something has shifted, but it's still way too early to call it a relationship. I've always enjoyed Amanda's company and how level-headed she is, especially coming from such a privileged upbringing. I love the way she wants to forge her own way, yet she still has a heart of gold and cares deeply about the mission of the James Blake Foundation and the homeless people their foundation helps."

"You're right about that, Peter. Amanda is an amazing woman. One word of caution though: if you hurt my friend, I'll sink your sailboat, so tread lightly."

Peter walked over to hand Cassidy a cup of freshly brewed coffee. "I promise I'll be careful. You know I love that boat and there's no way I want to give you justification to sink it. I promise to tread lightly."

Cassidy and Peter were lost in their individual thoughts for several minutes as they both continued to do prep work for the brunch. Several of the extra staff they hired for the day were starting to arrive, so Peter went into the dining room to get them organized, leaving Cassidy with her thoughts.

"Good morning...and a penny for your thoughts," Trish called from across the room. "I trust you and Jack enjoyed the rest of your evening?"

"Good morning to you also. We have a lot of work to do this morning so let's get at it and we can catch up later," Cassidy replied.

"Oh no you don't. I see that dreamy look on your face and don't think that I'm going to wait for hours to hear how you're feeling about everything that happened last night. That's no way to treat your best friend. If the tables were turned, you know you wouldn't let me rest until we talked about it."

The determined look on Trish's face made it clear to Cassidy that waiting was not an option. "Okay. Yes, we had a wonderful night. It's all still too new to sort out in my head, but my heart is a totally different matter. I didn't even realize how strong my feelings were for Jack until he took me in his arms and kissed me like I've never been kissed in my life."

"You may not have known it, but it was clear to me and Amanda that you were falling for Jack—you can't hide something like that from your best friends." Trish reached over and gave Cassidy a big hug and then went back to gathering linens and placing them on a cart.

Cassidy chopped away at a large bowl of green peppers. "All of that pent-up emotion and frustration just came rushing at me and before I knew it, I was 'weak in the knees,' as Grams would have said."

Trish still probed for more information. "Have you spoken to Jack yet this morning?"

"Not yet. He knows how important the brunch is for us today. Not only for the VIP guests but for the other brunch guests. We agreed that we'd wait until after the majority of the VIP guests check out later today. We planned to walk into town after the Sit-n-Sip tonight and find a place to talk. I know we have a lot to discuss. There are still some gaps in what I assumed was going on versus the reality, but I'm certain we can sort it all out."

Trish was stacking various sizes of plates onto a cart when they heard giggling coming from the hallway. "What was that? I thought I heard someone laughing but that would be odd since it's the hallway to the private residences." Trish left the cart where it was and walked quietly towards the door leading to the hallway. Not sure what she would find on the other side of the door, she slowly cracked it open, just enough to see into the hallway. Then, just as quickly, she quietly closed the door.

Trish walked back over to Cassidy who continued to prep food. When Cassidy saw the smile on Trish's face, she was curious about what she had seen.

"What's going on? Since we don't have any children at the inn this weekend, I can't imagine who would be in the hallway giggling," Cassidy said.

"It's Peter and Amanda. *Kissing*, by the way. Things clearly changed between them last night. They seemed way too cozy."

Cassidy stopped what she was doing to take a good look at Trish's face and body language. How did Trish feel about Peter and Amanda getting together? They had all been such good friends. Was Trish disappointed that Peter hadn't picked her? Would this hurt their overall friendship? And would she feel left out now that Cassidy *and* Amanda both had a love interest?

"Trish, how would you feel about Peter and Amanda moving into a romantic relationship? It's always been the four of us?" Cassidy questioned.

"It took me by surprise at first last night when I saw how closely they were dancing but the more I thought about it, I realized I've seen this coming for a while. Those two are well suited for each other and I'm happy Amanda found a good guy. As we all know, she's dated at least one guy that was only out for her money and the influence her father could bring to the table. Peter is as independent as Amanda is. I'm excited for them and, no, I don't feel hurt at all," Trish said as a big smile spread across her face.

Cassidy reached over and placed her arm through Trish's. "You are a great friend to all of us. It takes an incredibly good friend to only want what's best for their friends. I know your knight in shining armor is out there somewhere and I, for one, want to help you find him."

And then it hit her, and Cassidy continued. "By the way, guess who my limo driver was last night?"

Trish was folding napkins and didn't stop what she was doing to respond. "I have no idea. Who?"

"Derrick Williams. His friend owns the limo company and Derrick helps him out when he's not on duty. He also mentioned that the current Chief of Police is retiring. Now that he obtained his advanced degree in Criminal Justice Administration, he is being considered to replace the Chief. Didn't you have a big crush on him back in high school?"

Trish stopped folding the napkins, but she didn't look over at Cassidy. "Maybe I had a small crush on Derrick, but it never went anywhere. When he left Lakeview to go to college, we lost touch. I see him around town every so often, but he acts like he doesn't even know me." Trish suddenly smirked. "Cassidy, I see that look on your face. You know how you hate it when your mother plays matchmaker. Please, promise me you are not brewing something up in that flaky head of yours. I am absolutely not interested in Derrick Williams."

Cassidy rolled her eyes and Trish changed the subject back to the prior evening. "I still laugh when I think about how you and Jack were all tangled up on that sofa. I wish I had thought to take a picture. It would look fantastic on the front page of the *Lakeview Gazette* this morning with all the other pictures from the gala."

Trish looked over at Cassidy just in time to see a kitchen towel come flying at her.

"Okay," Trish said. "If you stop, I'll stop. We need to get back to work before Peter returns and sees that we're not done with setting the tables in the dining room."

They both laughed and returned to the prep work. Several minutes later Amanda and Peter returned to the kitchen. Of course, there were several rounds of good-natured teasing thrown around between the four friends, but in the end, duty called and they all jumped in to arrange the buffet. For the next several hours they were so busy they forgot about everything else, except for ensuring their guests had a delicious meal.

Once the gourmet brunch was over and the guests went back to their rooms to prepare for checking out, the four friends returned to the kitchen. "Fantastic job, everyone," Cassidy said. "I know I don't say this enough, but I couldn't pull any of this off without you. Peter, the food was out of this world. Trish and Amanda, the service was seamless. I know that Grams is looking down on us with a big smile today."

Peter added, "Cassidy, not only would Grams be smiling, but she'd also be enormously proud of you and what you've accomplished. This was your dream and you made it come true." Peter grabbed one of the champagne bottles meant for mimosas and filled four glasses. "Let's raise our glasses in a toast to Cassidy and to the success she's made of the Crystal Lake Inn. Cheers!"

Cassidy had blocked off all new reservations for two days after the VIP weekend so the crew could get things back in order. The inn was eerily quiet on Sunday evening, with the only guests being Jack, Amanda and Trish. Amanda and Trish had decided to stay until Monday afternoon so they could help Cassidy. Jack's reservation was up in a few days, but he had yet to indicate if he was staying longer or not. This worried Cassidy, but she felt it was too soon to mention it.

With the brunch cleanup finally completed, the four friends decided to go to their individual rooms and relax for a bit. Cassidy had invited them and Jack to their own private Sit-n-Sip on the front porch that evening, but for now, she was exhausted.

Putting the last of the dishes in the dishwasher, Cassidy headed to her suite and plopped down in her favorite reading chair, putting her feet up on the ottoman.

It had been a whirlwind few weeks, for sure. Cassidy looked at the clock and saw that she had time for a nap, so she set her phone to wake her in two hours. Her mind was going in circles and she needed some sleep to help clear her head. While still thinking through everything that had happened last night, her head bobbed over to one side and she drifted off to sleep.

Cassidy woke as a noise startled her. She realized that it was a light tapping on her door. *Who could that be?* she wondered. "I'm coming," Cassidy said a bit irritably to whoever this was waking her up from a perfectly good nap.

Opening the door Cassidy was surprised to see her mother standing there.

"Mom, what brings you here? Is something wrong?"

Kate stood there for a few seconds. Now that she was in front of Cassidy, she wasn't sure how to begin. She needed to explain to her daughter about knowing Jack's true identity, yet not sharing it with her.

Kate looked at her beautiful daughter and she momentarily thought of her first husband, Cassidy's father. Cassidy resembled him a bit, but she more so looked like Kate's mother, Adelaide. They shared the same height, their big brown doe-like eyes, and their strong independence. When Adelaide died, Cassidy was crushed, and it took several years for Kate and Cassidy to become as close as they were now. Kate worked hard to always be there when Cassidy needed her, but she also tried not to hover too much. All of these thoughts were rushing through her mind as she picked her words carefully.

"Hello, my darling daughter. I hope it's okay to stop by without calling. Duncan drove me over and dropped me off. He's in town having a quick meeting with a few of the VIP guests about the next steps for the hospital's new wing so I thought I'd stop by so we could talk. There are a few things I want to tell you."

"Okay, Mom." Cassidy opened her door wide for her mom to come in. As she rubbed her sleepy eyes, Kate thought how innocent and childlike her daughter looked, and it took her back in time for a moment. But she also saw the strong and fiercely independent woman Cassidy had become. For some strange reason, the image of bookends popped into Kate's head. Two bookends, each at the opposite end of the shelf, yet together they held a wide range of books, experience, emotions and opportunities. Maybe Cassidy was ready to open herself up to a new chapter in her life.

"Can I offer you something to drink or a snack?"

"No dear. I'm fine. I just have a few things I want to clear up with you and I need to do it now," Kate said but she felt a bit unsure of herself. Cassidy motioned for her mom to sit across from her in the little sitting area of her suite.

"As you are aware, Thornton Reed and I go way back to our college days. We have a special friendship and have been there for each other through many ups and downs in our

198

lives. As an executive and top publisher at Patterson Publishing Company, Thornton often provides signed copies of books from his authors. As you are also aware, Patterson has been an extremely generous donor to several of my charitable efforts over the years.

"When he agreed to give us signed copies from his latest best-selling author, Thomas J. Burnett, I was excited. I'll also admit that I saw the author's jacket photo, and the fact that he is a handsome and eligible bachelor didn't hurt either. Since Thornton's wife was out of the country on business, I asked him to bring along the author to the gala. And, yes, I had planned to switch around the table seating arrangements to put Thomas, or Jack, or whichever name he goes by, next to you at dinner. I feel so guilty about trying to play matchmaker again. I wanted to come clean. I'm so sorry about that. I promise I'll never do it again." She quickly used her finger to cross her heart.

Kate paused to see if Cassidy was going to explode, but her daughter remained silent so Kate continued. "I didn't realize that the author was staying at your inn until Thornton called me a few days ago and started asking questions. Thornton was with Jack in their New York office when they discovered the connection and called me to clarify if you were my daughter and if you were indeed the owner of the Crystal Lake Inn. He also confirmed that the author was staying here."

Cassidy interrupted her mother, "but Mom, I told you I had a guest from New York that was a bit challenging, don't you recall that conversation?"

"Now that you mention it, I do recall the conversation about the odd guest but you never mentioned his name or any other details so there wasn't anything to connect the two together."

"When did you realize that Thomas J. Burnett and the guest in Room #5 were the same person?" Cassidy asked.

"Last night, just as you did. But once I made the connection, I couldn't figure out why you were so mad and ran out of the room. Now it all seems to make sense."

Cassidy stared at her mother for a few seconds, "I'm glad it all makes sense to you because I was still confused about a few things, but you just cleared up the last details."

"If I'm not mistaken from what I saw throughout the evening, it seemed that you and Jack are very fond of each other. Am I right?"

"I'm still in a bit of shock, but yes, Mother. I'm very fond of Jack. At first, I was terribly hurt that he didn't share his identity with me, but once he explained everything, I understood. If I hadn't let my emotions get the best of me, I would have seen that Jack and I truly had a connection. Actually, it was like sparks every time we were together."

Kate walked over to her daughter and gave her a big hug.

"I'm so happy for you. You've protected your heart for so long but now is the time to let someone special in and I think that Jack is that person. Open your heart and let it be your guide." Kate hesitated. "What is next for you two?" she asked. "Jack lives in the city and you run an inn five hours away. While I want you to explore this relationship, I don't want to see you get hurt."

Cassidy was lost deep in thought for a few moments before responding, "I'm not totally sure where this is headed, but I plan to see it through. I can't overcome a five-hour difference in our home bases, but I know in my heart that Jack is that someone special for me. He makes my heart sing, my pulse race, and everything seem brighter."

"Oh, that sounds a bit more serious than I thought. Either way, you two need to sit down and have an honest conversation about your future."

Another knock at the door interrupted their conversation. There seemed to be a lot of traffic at Cassidy's door today.

Cassidy walked across the room hoping it was Jack, but instead it was Duncan, impeccably dressed in a navy-blue suit, crisp white shirt and dark leather dress shoes.

"I came to collect your mother, but I'm glad I had a minute to talk to you also. I was a bit worried about you when you raced out of the ballroom last night. Since then, your mother filled in the gaps of the story for me. Once you returned to the ballroom, you and Mr. Burnett seemed to be inseparable. I hope that is good news and I wish you the best. But, if you need someone to warn him not to hurt you, I'm your man," Duncan added with a big smile.

Cassidy's heart melted at the thought of her stepfather standing up to Jack on her behalf. While Duncan was physically fit for his age, he was about thirty years Jack's senior and about six inches shorter. "That is so sweet of you Duncan. I don't think I'll be needing that right now, but if something changes, I'll let you know," Cassidy reached over and gave her mother and Duncan a big hug.

The three said their goodbyes and Kate and Duncan left Cassidy alone again, with her thoughts.

Cassidy knew that a nap was now out of the question, so she jumped into the shower. She took extra time with her hair and makeup and changed her top another time or two before heading to the kitchen to get things ready for the Sit-n-Sip with Jack and her friends.

Cassidy was eagerly looking forward to some time with her friends and with Jack, although she was a bit nervous to see him again. How would he act toward her? Would they continue their closeness from the night before? At the brunch they had maintained a friendly yet professional manner, which almost drove Cassidy crazy. All she wanted to do was to walk into Jack's arms and let him hold her tight. At the end of the brunch, he'd had a meeting with Thornton, so she hadn't been able to see him alone. The Sit-n-Sip would be their first opportunity.

After Cassidy finished pulling the drinks and snacks together, she pushed the cart onto the porch. A terrible thought crossed her mind. What if Jack didn't join them? What if he'd had time to think it through and he realized he didn't feel the same way today? As usual, she was letting her negative thoughts take over and it was making her miserable.

Cassidy was a few minutes late arriving on the front porch so she knew everyone should already be there. She could slightly hear voices but couldn't tell who was speaking. Cassidy suddenly stopped at the front door. If Jack was on the porch, then everything would be fine. If he wasn't then her heart would break. She felt like her feet were glued to the floor—she couldn't move.

She heard Trish call her name and the front door opened. Trish was saying something to Cassidy but all she heard were mumbled words. She didn't hear Jack's voice among those on the front porch. He must have changed his mind. He wasn't joining them. Cassidy's world stopped spinning. She would be crushed if Jack decided to walk away. She was terrified to walk through the door but knew she had to—it was the moment of truth.

CHAPTER 19

Walking onto the porch, Cassidy immediately looked to the left and saw Amanda and Peter. She looked to the right and saw...Jack. Yes, Jack was there waiting for her. She didn't realize she had been holding her breath and let out a long, slow exhale of relief. Cassidy settled the cart along the wall and started to pour drinks for everyone. When she finally got up the nerve to look over at Jack, he had crossed the distance between them and was standing beside her.

"Cassidy, let me help you with those drinks and then we can sit down and relax. The four of you deserve it," Jack smiled and took drinks to Peter and Amanda, while Cassidy took a drink to Trish.

The group continued to make small talk, mainly about the previous night, until evening started to descend. They quietly watched the sky begin to turn a beautiful mix of light pinks and purples as the sun lowered toward the horizon. This was a beautiful time of day at the lake. Most visitors to Lakeview were either in their hotel rooms or already in town having dinner, which left the lake front almost empty. You could still hear the sound of activity at the docks as people came back from a long day of paddle boarding, kayaking and canoeing. Due to the lack of wind, the lake looked like glass and the reflection of the setting sun sparkled on the water.

As the colors deepened into dusk, the group decided to call it a day. Peter and Amanda offered to drop Trish off at home on their way to dinner at a small café on the outskirts of town. After everyone said their goodbyes and hugged each other, Jack and Cassidy stood on the porch and waved to their friends.

Jack surprised Cassidy by pulling her into his arms. "Are you ready to walk into town and grab dinner?"

"Actually, if it's okay with you, I'd rather heat up some leftovers from brunch and have a casual meal in the kitchen."

"That is more than okay with me," Jack said, a big smile crossing his face. Jack helped Cassidy put the cart back in the utility closet and while she heated up a light meal for them, he helped by setting the table.

Cassidy set the food on the table but before she could sit down Jack was next to her holding out his arms.

"I couldn't resist one more kiss before we eat. I've been patiently waiting for hours to kiss you," Jack said quietly into her ear.

It took several more kisses before they finally sat down to eat. Over dinner they talked through a few more questions Cassidy had for Jack, mainly about how his book was coming and if all the legal issues with his contract had been worked out, which he confirmed they had been.

"Amazingly, I'm almost finished with the rough draft. I need a few more long days of writing and I'll be ready to email it to Thornton. Once I do that, I'll have a few days with a lot of free time until he gets the necessary edits back to me. What does your schedule look like the rest of this week? I know you're busy tomorrow, but would it be possible for you to carve out some time for the two of us to spend together?"

"I'd love to spend some quality time with you Jack, but this inn is more than a full-time job. I'll have to see what I can work out. It will be a bit easier now that Peter is back, and I think Amanda may have a special incentive to spend more time here. That being said, I'm very motivated to make it work." She grinned mischievously. "Let me talk to Peter in the morning."

Jack and Cassidy spent the next two hours sitting on the porch, enjoying the summer evening. The porch swing was the perfect place to sit, listen to the lake water hit against the rocks and watch people take an evening stroll along the walkway. Since the swing was at the end of the porch, out of the way of the lights, it was also the perfect place to steal a few kisses without being noticed by anyone walking by the inn.

It was a wonderful evening and Cassidy was lulled into a sense of peacefulness and contentment. She laid her head on Jack's shoulder and before she realized it, she was fast asleep.

Cassidy wasn't sure how long Jack let her sleep curled up against him, but she heard him softly calling her name.

"Oh my, I'm so embarrassed, Jack. I can't believe I fell asleep." Cassidy looked at her watch and saw that over an hour had passed. "Why didn't you wake me up?"

Jack brushed her hair out of her face and kissed her lips lightly. "You looked so peaceful. I enjoyed having you snuggled up against me."

Cassidy tried to cover a yawn, but it snuck out. "I hate to call it a night, but I'm bushed and need to get some sleep. Since you are officially our only guest, we'll just have a continental breakfast around nine o'clock in the morning. Trish and Amanda will be here along with the cleaning crew. Will you be down for breakfast?"

"Yes, if you agree not to attack me with the vacuum cleaner cord this time. Afterwards, I plan to try and knock out as much of my final chapter as possible. I doubt if I'll come up for air or even for dinner. If I'm lucky and keep at it, I might be able to wrap it up by Tuesday afternoon. Will that give you time to figure out if you can take the day off on Wednesday? Peter offered us the use of his boat for the day and the weather forecast predicts it will be the perfect day for sailing."

"Peter loaned you his boat? That's a first. Do you even know how to handle a sailboat that size?"

"For your information, young lady, Peter and I first met at our university sailing club. Yes, I not only know how to handle his boat, but I have one, slightly larger, of my own. Regrettably, it hardly gets used these days. I plan to change that if my plans work out the way I hope they will."

"What do you mean if your plans work out?" Cassidy questioned Jack.

"Oh, nothing specific just yet. Let me know about Wednesday so I can tell Peter."

Jack pulled Cassidy into another hug and a deep, passionate kiss. Cassidy knew that the lack of guests at the inn was letting both of their minds race to places they shouldn't. It was too soon for either of them, but the thought of doing more than just kissing crossed both their minds.

In a voice just above a whisper Jack said, "If I don't let you go right now, I think we may do something we're not ready for at this point, but don't think it hasn't crossed my mind all evening. One more kiss and I'll say goodnight."

Cassidy had just slipped into bed when there was a knock on her door. She froze for a second. On one hand she hoped it was Jack. On the other hand, she wasn't sure she wanted it to be Jack. She walked over and slowly opened it.

"I know it's late, but I wanted to speak with you for a minute if it's okay?" Peter stood at the door with his hands stuffed in his pockets, a worried expression on his face.

"Of course, come on in." Cassidy turned on a few lights and grabbed her robe. "What's on your mind, Peter?"

"I thought we should talk about everything that happened over the past few days. I feel badly that I didn't get to you before the gala to tell you that the guest in Room

#5 was my old college buddy and that he was a writer of international spy novels. The day of the gala was so hectic. You were in town at the salon, and we kept missing each other. I hope you're not mad at me."

"Oh, Peter, I'm so over all of that now. My mother also stopped by to say she was sorry she hadn't put two and two together and warned me. It now seems so silly that I didn't make the connection on my own."

Cassidy walked over to the table by her door and picked up Jack's novel. "If I only had taken a bit of time and started reading this book, I would have figured it all out weeks ago. It's a good lesson to me about taking time for myself."

It seemed like Peter was about to say something but then changed his mind and headed to the door. He stopped abruptly, turned back toward Cassidy and sat down in her favorite reading chair.

"Cassidy, you and I have been close friends and business associates for years. That type of friendship brings with it a certain sense of responsibility for the happiness of your friends. It also teaches you that sometimes it's better to keep your opinions to yourself. In this case, I'll throw caution to the wind and give you some advice." Peter paused to see if Cassidy was going to interrupt him.

When she didn't, Peter continued, "you are a great friend. You take care of the needs of others before your own. When one of us is sick you're the first one to tell us to stay in bed and then you run yourself ragged tending to our needs. When we hurt, you hurt. When we cry, you bring us the entire box of tissues. You love this inn and you've put your heart and soul into it. You strive to make every guest feel special and you go out of your way to find unique ways to exceed their expectations."

"Peter, you're making me embarrassed," Cassidy quickly interjected. "Yes, I care a lot about this inn and my friends. Is there anything wrong with that?"

"Yes, there is when you always put yourself lower down on the priority list. When is the last time you took a real vacation? Or more importantly right now, when is the last time you let a man into your life romantically? I've seen you push men away when things start to get too serious. It seems to me that Jack is interested in you. Please don't push him away. You and he both deserve a chance to see where this goes. Be open to this new journey Cassidy."

Cassidy could feel Peter's eyes watching for her reaction. In her heart she knew Peter was right. In her head she could feel that little inner critic telling her to be careful not to get her heart broken.

After a few moments Cassidy replied. "Thank you for being such a good friend. I'm not sure when you got so wise, but I hear the wisdom in your words. It's my nature to put everyone else first and that is a big part of what made this inn a success. You've opened my eyes to the fact that I also, occasionally, use this place to hide behind. I promise to give your comments more thought. It may be time I do a bit of reprioritizing and put myself first occasionally. Will that make you happy?"

"The real question is not if that will make *me* happy. The real question is will that make *you* happy Cassidy? Will a relationship with Jack make you happy? I don't expect you to answer that question tonight. It's a question that you need to honestly think through because if you're only going to push Jack away in a week or two, end it now and minimize the hurt both of you will face. If, on the other hand, you can be open to the possibility of more, then go for it. Find a way to spend some quality time with him and see where it leads."

Peter got up from the chair, walked over to the bed where Cassidy was sitting and planted a brotherly kiss on her forehead. He headed toward the door.

Before he reached it Cassidy called him to come back in. "Peter, speaking of spending some quality time with Jack, did you offer him your sailboat for the full day? I've never known you to let anyone use your precious boat."

"Yes, I did offer Jack the boat. I know he's skilled in the art of sailing. I think it will do you two good to get away all to yourselves. By the way, I owe you big time for filling in for me while I went to help my mother. Amanda, Trish and I talked about it tonight and we want to give you the rest of the week off starting on Wednesday. You wouldn't need to be back until the following Tuesday. You and Jack can either spend it all together and get away from Lakeview or you can decide to spend it alone. Whatever you decide, you should do it away from the inn. You've been going at it for years. It's time for a break."

Peter reached over and gave Cassidy a hug. She almost burst into tears of happiness. "I don't know what to say. That is so generous of the three of you! You know we have a full house next week. That might make it a bit tough on all of you. Jack asked me tonight if I might be able to get away for a few days so that we could get to know each other better. I wasn't sure at the time if I wanted to take him up on his offer, but I've come to realize that I'd love to be able to do that if you're sure you guys can handle everything around here."

"Absolutely, let's finalize the plans at breakfast tomorrow. I'm beat and need to get some sleep. At least we can all sleep late tomorrow. See you in the morning," Peter called as he headed out the door.

Cassidy was on cloud nine. This was such a generous offer by her friends and it's what she and Jack needed—time to get to know each other better. Her feelings for Jack were growing by the minute. She was falling fast and hard.

Cassidy reached over to turn off the bedside lamp but before she could even get the light turned off, there was another knock on her door. *Again?* Her room was starting to feel like Grand Central Station. She assumed Peter forgot to tell her something, so she jumped out of bed and yanked the door open. When she saw Jack at her door and not Peter, Cassidy froze.

"I know it's extremely late and I also know that I shouldn't have come to your room like this, but I couldn't help myself. I also know what I'm about to say isn't something I *should* say either. Cassidy, I think I'm falling in love with you. You are everything I've ever wanted in a woman and a life partner. You are a fantastic businesswoman, strong and independent, yet so sweet and loving. Every time I kiss you, my heart soars and I lose all sensibility. You have me under your spell."

Cassidy backed up and Jack walked into the room, pulled Cassidy into his arms and tenderly kissed her until she felt like she was floating.

"Jack...it's a bad idea for you to be here and I agree that you shouldn't already be telling me these things, but if I'm being honest, I was dying all night to tell you the same thing. I'm falling for you too. It's not like me. I typically approach a relationship very slowly and cautiously. But you are driving me crazy, Mr. Burnett."

Jack looked thoughtfully at Cassidy and then said, "I had a long-term relationship once. We took our time and got to know each other really well. After two years of dating, we moved in together and planned to get married. We had a large group of mutual friends, we liked the same restaurants, the same vacation spots and I *thought* we were in total alignment regarding our future together." Jack paused for a second and then continued, "and then she found someone else. It doesn't seem that taking it slowly is any more successful than knowing when it's right. All I know is that you've stolen my heart and I want to be with you tonight."

Cassidy paused for a split second before she said, "Jack, you've stolen my heart too. My Grams always told me I'd know when my knight in shining armor came along. He'd steal my heart, make mush of my brain and make my legs weak when he kissed me. So far, you're three for three. Yes, I want you to stay with me tonight."

Cassidy reached over and turned out the lamp. The moon was so bright it provided just enough illumination for

Cassidy to see Jack's face. A shaft of light found its way through the small crack in the window curtains and hit the white of his shirt, making it nearly shine. It struck Cassidy that Jack truly was her knight in shining armor.

EPILOGUE

It was a gorgeous Autumn day. The green leaves of summer had already started their procession into vibrant yellows, oranges, and reds. The daytime weather was still warm, but the early morning hour required Cassidy to wear a light jacket. As she walked along the trail around the lake, Cassidy thought back over the past six months and how much her life had changed.

Cassidy recalled doing this same walk among the brilliantly colored autumn leaves many years ago. Up ahead she saw the same bench on which she and Grams sat and planned out the renovations for the inn. She sat down on the bench and looked out at the smooth waters of the lake.

Cassidy clearly recalled Grams' excitement at the proposal to overhaul the main rooms and how she added her exquisite taste to redecorate the community room and the dining room. Grams felt that these two rooms, along with the lobby, were among the most important rooms to make guests immediately feel welcome and comfortable.

A smile spread across Cassidy's face at the plans they made that day. Cassidy had worked extremely hard to fulfill their goals and dreams. In some instances, she'd been able to go way beyond what they had envisioned. She wondered if Grams was proud of what she'd been able to accomplish. She sure hoped so.

This glorious morning was the last one Cassidy would have as a single woman. The glow she felt inside seemed to radiate like the sun reflecting off the lake that day. This was her last quiet time before all the chaos of a wedding day, but it was hard to remain calm. She was so excited to marry her knight in shining armor. Cassidy couldn't wait another day to marry Jack.

Over the past six months, they had grown closer, and their relationship had strengthened. They had had a romantic and wonderfully relaxing week on Peter's sailboat. Jack was a wonderful sailor and helmsman and along the way he'd taught Cassidy how to help hoist the sails and prepare the boat for the evenings when they docked at various ports along the New England coastline.

They had hours and hours to get to know each other better and plenty of time to work through the many hurdles and challenges they faced. As Cassidy thought about what it took for them to get to this day, she was amazed it had all worked out so well.

Jack finished his third book only two weeks after the gala. Once it was released it quickly became another bestseller. Per his contract, Jack had to head back to New York and then fly to a number of other cities to do book tours and media appearances, but he always came back to Lakeview between engagements.

Thornton Reed had been a good friend to them both. He and Jack worked out a deal that made it easy for Jack to relocate to Lakeview. In return, Jack agreed he would return to the city when necessary to fulfill his obligations. Thornton also got Jack to agree to another series, but only after he and Cassidy were married and took their honeymoon.

Jack moved into the inn, but after a few months he and Cassidy found a cute little cottage down the street which had big picture windows on the first and second floors that overlooked the lake. They renovated the cottage, and a room on the second floor with a balcony overlooking the lake was perfect for Jack's office. The setting gave him the peace he needed to write and the views to let his imagination flow.

Originally, Cassidy was concerned about moving out of the inn, but ultimately, she found that living close by worked perfectly to give her and Jack some privacy and provide her some much needed balance in her life. She could be at the inn in less than five minutes if needed.

As for the management of the inn, Amanda stepped up and asked Cassidy to consider letting her take on more responsibilities. It seemed Amanda and her father had sorted out their differences and he offered to hire someone else to run the family foundation, James Blake Charities, while Amanda provided oversight.

So, Cassidy agreed she and Amanda would manage the inn together. For the past several months things were running smoothly, and business was better than ever. Amanda's operational excellence streamlined costs yet made the daily running of the inn much easier.

Another surprise was the deepening relationship between Peter and Amanda. They not only moved in together, but they also tore down the wall between Cassidy's suite and the extra guest suite to make a large apartment out of the two spaces. They remodeled the entire space, enlarged the kitchen and added a private deck, where they constantly entertained their friends. Peter's former suite was turned into the extra guest suite. It was often used by visiting family or friends. Sometimes when Jack was out of town on long book tours, Cassidy would stay in the guest suite. Amanda and Trish often joined her for a girls' sleepover— just like they used to have in the old days. Amazingly, Peter understood the tight friendship of the three women, and he typically provided them with a delicious meal or snacks.

Cassidy also thought back to the night of the Lakeview Hospital Gala. She laughed out loud when she thought of the chain of events that happened that night. She also chuckled to herself now as she recalled throwing those pointy-toed high heels she wore that night in the inn's donation bin—never to be worn on her feet again.

Thinking of the hospital, Cassidy was amazed at how quickly the Neonatal Unit was being built. The outside walls were already erected, and the project was on target to be completed in another year. Her mother continued her fundraising to make sure that all of the specialty equipment was installed and ready to go on day one.

Cassidy's final thought as she gazed out over the lake from her bench was about the special times she and Jack had spent together. With Amanda helping to run the inn, Cassidy was able to join Jack on several of his book tours. When possible, they took time to sightsee and enjoy some private time along the way.

While Cassidy always tried to stay in the background, occasionally an energetic reporter would thrust a camera and microphone in front of her. The most common question asked: "How did you manage to snag the most eligible bachelor in New York?" Jack typically jumped in to say that he was the one who was lucky enough to hook Cassidy and that it had taken a lot of persuasion to get her to fall in love with him. She loved when he made those types of comments.

Looking at her watch, Cassidy saw that it was time for her to return to the inn to get dressed. She gazed one last time at the gorgeous late Autumn day around her and marveled at how fitting it was that her wedding was on a day similar to the one she spent with Grams several years prior. Maybe all of the most important events of her life would happen on gorgeous Autumn days. She'd keep that in mind when making big decisions.

Just as Cassidy started to get up from the bench, a single ray of sunshine burst through the tree line and lit the Autumn leaves, magically turning them into a magnificent bouquet of fall hues. The beauty almost took Cassidy's breath away. Suddenly, Cassidy felt a chill on her arms. She dared not move but sat so still she could hear the faint wind blowing off the lake.

Cassidy smiled as she felt like she could hear Grams softly saying to her…. *"Get moving Cassidy, it's time for you to marry your knight. It's another day to live your life, do good in the world and yes, you've made me proud. Oh, and remember to smile!"*

Everyone was talking at once. Cassidy looked around the room at the small group. Her mother looked beautiful in a navy blue tea-length gown embellished with a lace overlay across the bodice. Amanda and Trish had bought matching dresses in coordinating earth tones, perfect for an Autumn setting. Sarah Jennings, the local artisan who made many of the special items the inn sold to their guests, was also there making final adjustments to the bouquets the women would be carrying. As a special touch, Sarah had hand-painted a picture of the inn on the bright orange ribbons tied around each bouquet. They were beautiful.

Sarah had also set up an arbor in the garden of the inn with the same golden mums, vibrant burgundy dahlias and yellow roses to match the flowers in the bouquets, and pale orange ribbon draped at the end of each row of chairs. All in all, about twenty-five guests were in attendance.

Kate had pushed for a larger wedding, but Cassidy and Jack insisted on a small event with just their closest family and friends. They wanted their special day to truly be *their* special day. Of course, Kate added several small touches that made the setting absolutely gorgeous. Tall flickering candles were placed around the garden and thousands of mini fairy lights cast a warm glow over the entire yard.

Peter insisted on providing the food and he spared no expense. The meal was absolutely fabulous. Even for the small group, he insisted on a seated dinner with filet mignon, lobster and all the trimmings.

The women had gathered to do each other's hair and makeup. Amanda, Trish, Sarah and Kate had showered Cassidy with gifts, posed for photos and then had a champagne toast.

After everyone else left the room following the toast, Kate walked over to Cassidy and said, "It's time for us to go outside for the big moment."

Mother and daughter gazed into the full-length mirror set up in the room at the inn and looked at their reflection…Cassidy was radiant with her long hair pulled up into a chignon with a white pearl beaded barrette holding it off her neck. But it was the dress that took their breath away. The all white gown was made of soft chiffon and delicate lace with a scoop neckline and cap sleeves. The A-Line silhouette was perfect for Cassidy's petite frame while the flowing train and the line of tiny pearl buttons running down the back made the perfect finish to the absolutely gorgeous gown. The navy-blue of Kate's dress made the crisp white wedding gown even more stunning. Mother and daughter took a minute to appreciate their reflection and like a flower you dry and press to save forever, they committed the view in the mirror to their special memories.

"You look so lovely. I can't believe this day is finally here," Kate told Cassidy. "Before we go downstairs, I have one more gift for you. It's something I was entrusted with many years ago and asked to give to you on this special day."

"Mom, you and Duncan already gave me these beautiful diamond earrings and necklace along with the use of your cabin for a month for our honeymoon. What more could you have to give me? You've already been so generous."

Kate walked over to her purse and pulled out a small beautifully wrapped package and handed it to Cassidy. "Open it, my dear."

Cassidy carefully opened the package and tears formed in her eyes when she saw the contents. Pulling out the gift she carefully unfolded the delicate hanky. It was yellowed with age, but it was clearly embroidered with her grandmother's initials. A note card simply said, *Something old for your special day, love Grams.*

With tears in her eyes Kate said, "Grams gave this to me the day I married your father. She asked me to keep it in a safe place and give it to you on your wedding day. She hoped that you'd continue to hand it down to your firstborn child on his or her wedding day. I think it will fit perfectly inside the pocket you had the seamstress sew into the side of your skirt."

Cassidy held the hanky between her hands for a moment and then raised it to her nose. She thought she caught a whiff of the flowery perfume Grams always wore. Somehow Cassidy knew Grams wouldn't forget her on her special day. Cassidy reached down and carefully inserted the hanky into her pocket. Trying to hold back the tears threatening to fall, she leaned over and hugged her mother.

"It's the most precious gift of all. Thank you so much. This is truly the most wonderful day of my life. It's the most perfect wedding day any girl could ask for."

"Well, if you want to get married today we better get outside. Duncan is waiting at the bottom of the stairs so that both of us can escort you outside. And Duncan is over the moon that you asked him to walk you down the aisle. It was so sweet of you to ask him."

Five minutes later Cassidy walked down the aisle on Duncan's arm. When she saw Jack standing under the arbor she almost lost it.

She took a minute to just stare at her future husband. His three-piece tuxedo had a modern cut with a wide lapel and just a hint of satin running down the legs of his trousers. The stark white shirt, black bowtie and a row of tiny pearl-covered buttons on his shirt all added to the sophisticated look. Yet Jack looked way more relaxed than Cassidy felt. She'd never seen him look more irresistible. She told herself that she wasn't going to cry, so she bit her lip and put a big smile on her face.

After the minister asked who was giving her away, Jack walked over to shake hands with Duncan, and he gave Kate a big hug. Then Jack took Cassidy's hand and brought her to the arbor in front of the minister.

The minister started the ceremony, but all Cassidy could hear was the beating of her heart as she held Jack's hand and stared into those baby blue eyes. They were absolutely gorgeous. The strangest thought crossed her mind—she hoped their children had those same beautiful blue eyes.

The minister calling her name brought her out of her reverie. She and Jack had written their own vows and recited them, then they exchanged rings. Before she knew it, Jack reached over and pulled her into his chest for a wonderful embrace and kiss.

And just like that, she was Mrs. Thomas Jack Burnett.

Jack took her hand and they walked back up the aisle to create a receiving line to accept the well-wishes of their friends and family. Of course, Jack took every opportunity possible to lean over and give Cassidy a kiss.

"I'm starving," Jack said, grinning. "Getting married is hard work. Duncan, please say the blessing so we can eat." Then he guided Cassidy to the head table and Peter personally served them their dinner.

"This is delicious," Cassidy said, eating a forkful of lobster dipped in drawn butter. "I didn't realize how hungry I was until we sat down to eat. Please let me finish my dinner before we start to dance this time," Cassidy pleaded with Jack.

"Only if you share your steak with me. I already ate most of mine," Jack said with a sly smile on his face.

Cassidy took joy in cutting off a small piece of steak to feed to Jack from her fork. It was an intimate gesture that started a round of forks clinking on glasses to get them to kiss which they happily did—several times, in fact.

Once they were done with dinner the small orchestra started to play the song they agreed would be their first dance. It was an oldie that her mother and father had used for the first dance at their wedding many years prior. As the music began and Jack and Cassidy took to the dance floor installed especially for the wedding, Cassidy sought out her mother to see her reaction. She saw Kate stop talking and look toward the dance floor. When Kate and Cassidy's eyes met, Kate threw a big kiss toward her daughter. Cassidy could see her mother dabbing her eyes.

Cassidy looked up at Jack, "Thank you for agreeing to use this song for our first dance. It's special to my parents and we grew up listening to my mother sing it over and over."

"You might be surprised if you looked over at my parents right now. Most likely there will be tears in my mother's eyes also. This was one of their favorite songs. It seems that *We've Only Just Begun* by the Carpenters was a favorite at weddings in the seventies."

Just then the lyrics about *"white lace and promises,"* played and Cassidy hugged Jack tighter as they danced. They had just made promises to each other…and the white lace of Grams shawl fit perfectly.

Duncan came to dance with Cassidy and Jack moved over to dance with Kate. Minutes later, Duncan turned Cassidy over to Jack's father and Jack danced with his mother. As Cassidy danced with Jack's father she saw where his good looks came from. Both men were tall, had dark wavy hair and those big blue eyes.

Soon they were joined on the dance floor by their family and friends. Everyone seemed to be having a fabulous time.

Finally, the sun dropped below the tree line and the candles and twinkling lights made the yard look like a magical fairyland. It was breathtaking.

Hours later Jack and Cassidy were saying their goodbyes to everyone. They had changed into casual clothes. Peter and Amanda had already grabbed the suitcases Jack and

Cassidy packed earlier and put them into the car that was pulled up to the curb. For the trip up the mountain Jack had rented a large, bright red, four-wheel-drive Jeep. It wasn't as romantic as his cute little sports car, but it sure would handle the mountain roads much better.

With a last round of hugs and well wishes, the newly married couple jumped into the car and drove off.

Several hours later they arrived at Kate and Duncan's cabin. Kate had their local caretaker stock the pantry and refrigerator. The gas fireplace was on, and the cabin was warm and toasty.

When they got to the front door, Jack put down the suitcases and started to pick Cassidy up. "I may be old-fashioned, but I want to carry my bride over the threshold."

"As long as you don't drop me, I'm happy to let you carry me any time you get the urge to do it."

Jack unlocked the door, turned the knob and started to push open the door. He then lifted Cassidy into his arms and gave her a deep kiss. She rested her head against his chest.

All of a sudden, Cassidy felt Jack's chest moving up and down and she heard a loud laugh escape his lips. She looked up to see what was causing him to laugh during such a romantic moment. When Cassidy saw the brass plaque on the door she started to laugh as well.

After they both had a good laugh, Jack walked over the threshold and put his wife down with one more kiss. He removed his phone from his pocket and walked back over to the door. He took a picture of the sign, then sent a text to three people he assumed were waiting to hear from them.

As soon as the text was sent, Jack turned off the lights and walked his new wife down the hallway to the bedroom. Tonight was the start of their lives together—one they hoped would be filled with lots of passion, personal and professional successes, and if they were lucky, maybe a few little Burnetts running around the yard.

Life at Crystal Lake Inn was about to get even more exciting than ever. Both Jack and Cassidy were looking forward to every exciting, crazy, hectic and fun minute.

Back at the inn, three cell phones beeped at the same time. Peter, Amanda and Trish picked up their phones to see who was sending them a text after midnight. All of them burst out laughing. Peter said, "and it's a fitting end to a perfect wedding day. I think we are all bushed. Let's call it a night." And with that they walked into the inn.

Amanda took one last look at the screen on her phone and laughed again at the picture Jack sent to them. The picture showed the cabin's front door with a plaque hanging from a silky white ribbon. The few words printed on the plaque summed it all up perfectly: *ROOM #5—DO NOT DISTURB.*

THE END

Photo by Ryan Bouchard

ABOUT THE AUTHOR

Susan W. Green writes contemporary romance novels using lighthearted stories with strong female leads, showing how they overcome challenges and find true happiness. She loves a good cup of coffee, so don't be surprised to find coffee mentioned in each of her books.

Long-time residents of Delaware, Susan and her husband Earl found a run-down house in nearby Maryland. Loving a fixer-upper, they bought the house, did extensive renovations and now enjoy the peaceful views of rolling hills and farmland. An added perk—family next door.

Susan loves hosting family and friends and giving back. After retiring from a 35-year career in banking, she continues to stay busy by volunteering at multiple universities, entrepreneur programs, and as a board member for a charity that supports children and teen moms. If you can't find her behind her desk, look on her front porch where she has her favorite rocking chair. And of course, a cup of coffee in hand. For more information, visit www.booksbysusanwgreen.com

Crystal Lake Inn Word Search

G	T	E	L	Y	A	M	A	N	D	A	A	P	T
R	O	F	K	D	S	M	L	L	A	K	E	T	L
A	N	K	A	I	L	A	U	O	T	T	C	S	A
M	R	C	T	S	U	I	R	L	E	E	T	I	A
S	E	A	E	S	I	N	N	R	M	L	T	L	R
N	T	J	C	A	D	E	C	O	F	F	E	E	E
I	X	O	L	C	M	A	I	L	I	A	E	V	J
G	A	A	N	A	X	M	T	U	N	A	N	O	R
Y	B	L	E	S	A	L	A	G	O	N	C	N	X
O	A	C	O	N	N	E	L	L	Y	L	C	K	S
L	Y	O	R	A	B	L	U	E	E	Y	E	S	L
D	O	N	O	T	D	I	S	T	U	R	B	D	K
E	E	A	K	C	L	A	T	A	N	O	E	N	U
R	E	E	N	R	I	A	C	R	Y	S	T	A	L

CASSIDY	BAXTER	BLUE EYES
COFFEE	CRYSTAL	GRAMS
AMANDA	DO NOT DISTURB	JACK
MAINE	NOVELIST	INN
CONNELLY	LAKE	KATE
NEONATAL	GALA	PETER

Word Search created by Frankie Rowles

Made in the USA
Middletown, DE
08 June 2022